THE SILENCE OF GETHSEMANE

THE SILENCE
OF
GETHSEMANE

MICHEL BENOÎT

Translated from the French
by Christopher Moncrieff

ALMA BOOKS

ALMA BOOKS LTD
London House
243–253 Lower Mortlake Road
Richmond
Surrey TW9 2LL
United Kingdom
www.almabooks.com

Dans le silence des oliviers first published by Éditions Albin Michel in 2011
First published in English by Alma Books Limited in 2012
This mass-market edition first published by Alma Books Limited in 2013
Copyright © Michel Benoît, 2011
Translation © Christopher Moncrieff, 2012

This book is supported by the Institut Français
as part of the Burgess programme.

Liberté • Égalité • Fraternité
RÉPUBLIQUE FRANÇAISE

Printed in England by CPI Group (UK) Ltd, Croydon CR0 4YY

Typesetting and eBook version by Tetragon

ISBN: 978-1-84688-240-1
EBOOK: 978-1-84688-274-6

THE SILENCE OF GETHSEMANE

To Didier,
my far-distant brother.
And to Laurence.

Into Jesus's mouth I have put only those words that research suggests he was likely to have used. These are indicated by inverted commas. As for the thoughts and dialogues that I attribute to various individuals, I would like to think that they are a true reflection of my dedicated study of the ancient texts.

Part I

Born into Disquiet

The Demon is forever by my side;
He swirls around me, as elusive as the air I breathe...

Baudelaire

1

In the dark of the night I lean back against an olive tree.

The rugged strength of its trunk gives me a feeling almost akin to abiding friendship. At this moment, just before the beginning of the agony that those around me can sense is fast approaching, I have an obsessive need for closeness, something I have always lacked.

On the other side of the Kidron Valley, the vast shape of the Temple glows faintly in the light of the full, paschal moon. The dull murmur of the crowd of pilgrims who have come from every corner of the Empire to celebrate the greatest of Jewish festivals can just be heard in this olive grove planted on a slope that looks out across the city. For the first time since I was a boy, I am not among them. Gethsemane, an oil press nestling on the hillside, is the place I have chosen for my self-imposed exile.

My presence here tonight is a sign of my absence from Israel.

I like this garden, the trees that celebrate my coming with their shadows. We have been hiding here since the sun went down, when the High Priests and the Pharisees issued a warrant for my arrest. Among the bustle of the streets or on the Temple esplanade, the crowd of my admirers and opponents protects me: to arrest me in broad daylight would transform the fickle, volatile mob into a solid mass, united in their hatred of Caiaphas's police. Ever since

7

we returned to Jerusalem I have had to decline Lazarus's kind offers of hospitality, which would put him in jeopardy. From now on we will be spending our nights in the uncertain sanctuary of this olive grove.

Caiaphas is aware of this. If I am arrested, it will be done covertly, taking advantage of a moment such as this, when the human shield that surrounds me from dawn till dusk is no longer there to protect me.

Perhaps even tonight.

So are these the last moments of freedom that I shall enjoy?

Consumed by their personal schemes and disquiet, my disciples fell asleep on the carpet of dead leaves in a nearby clearing as soon as they wrapped themselves in their cloaks. Let them have their rest, these wakeful sleepers whose dreams of power have always prevented them from grasping what it is that I so wanted to offer my Jewish brethren and their threadbare Judaism!

Tonight, among all their deep-seated beliefs there is one that seems to expose human frailty in a way that is especially tragic: they have always been sure in their minds that death is the end of life. Yet for many years, Israel has had contact with peoples from the Orient who realize that it is nothing of the sort, that death is simply a moment in time when we pass over from one life to another. So before my present life I must have lived a great many others, whose details aren't worth trying to imagine – what good would it do? But when I draw my last breath, I hope that this death will be my last.

During the last two years while I have been teaching, I have paid little heed to my body. As a tireless walker I have asked a great deal of it, coming to know its limits, just how far I can push it before it weakens. Faced with days of constant wandering, unforeseen encounters and impediments, confrontations that became increasingly violent, I was vitality itself. Since my time in the wilderness I have been sustained by an inner strength that has never failed me. I have recently raised the subject of my violent death with my disciples, yet although it had always been predictable it was still a somewhat vague concept. The end of my life? In a sense it was a reality that existed outside of me.

Yet having defied the Temple authorities so many times, I am aware that they posed a risk to me: only recently I was warned not to come to this hornets' nest, Jerusalem. But some of my disciples – Peter, John and his brother, Judas, Simon – have remained in touch with the Zealots they know, while others are still close to the Essenes. In Galilee I have friends who are Pharisees, while the Judaean has influential contacts in Jerusalem itself.

So, ignoring the danger, I thought I was safe.

Until these last few days, that is, when I have seen Peter take Judas aside several times and talk to him at length. I have detected a change in Iscariot, who for the first time has started disagreeing with my decisions. This evening, too, out of the corner of my eye I saw Peter slip a short sword under the folds of his cloak, the sort carried by the Sicarii, fanatical Jews who are close to the Zealots and who never hesitate to use these weapons. During the meal I offered Judas a piece of bread from my dish, the traditional sign of friendship: he took it without a word, then suddenly got up and walked out of the upper room with a stony expression on his face.

The noose is tightening round my neck.

I have glimpsed the shadow of death.

I'm afraid.

Sharpened by the pressures of the last few days, perhaps released from its bonds by the strange silence that hangs over this garden, which is an island of tranquillity on the outskirts of the city and its throng of pilgrims, my memory relives various moments in my short life with extraordinary vividness. It is now clear that it is the culmination of an almost unbroken line of Jewish prophets. All of them tried to make the whisper of their prophet's instinct heard, to act as a counterpoint to the mighty bellow of the Law. I so wanted to be the fulfilment of this line, for my life to bring ancient Israel to its consummation.

Consummate... the Greeks, whose language isn't unfamiliar to me – in the Empire, everyone speaks some Greek – use the word *plérōma*. It has a sense of plenitude, of perfection (as well as the satisfaction that comes with it) that my native Aramaic isn't able to express.

I wanted to bring the Law and the lives of the prophets to a state of perfection: but I failed. My whole life has been a failure. The most insignificant general of some Roman legion will have a longer entry in the official chronicles of the Empire than I will. A mere vagrant from a Jewish province in the back of beyond, if the Roman historians even refer to my death it will be as an afterthought, without the slightest notion of what it was that I was trying to be or to achieve.

Eventually, I suppose, people will think of writing an account of the life I led among them after meeting John the Baptist. Just as they passed me by during my lifetime, after I'm dead they will alter what I said and did to suit their personal hopes and ambitions. They might even go so far as to turn me into something I never was.

Knowing people as I do, I can imagine the result.

2

I have never liked Jerusalem, this arrogant city where they put prophets to death. Throughout my childhood, as well as during these last few months of turmoil and excitement when I really believed that I was going to be able to achieve this fulfilment, I walked past them on the hills of Galilee that surround the lake, which although usually calm and tranquil is prone to sudden storms.

My Galilee! So provincial, so isolated from Jerusalem, with its grating dialect that city dwellers poke fun at, its hills and caves where terrorists still have their hideouts today, just as they did in King David's time. The pale, gentle gold of the crops in the fields, the warm water of the lake where my first companions earned their living! It wasn't me who chose these fishermen, it was they who found me, or at least the first four did. Andrew, Peter, Philip, Nathanael and – even before Andrew – the Judaean. It was at the mouth of the Jordan, near where John the Baptist was living. Sometimes I have had to keep away from its banks, mostly to avoid the minions of that sly old fox, King Herod. But always I returned, as if irresistibly drawn to the reflection of the sky in the surface of the water.

This is where I was born, in Capernaum – not Bethlehem as some people might suppose. And not in Nazareth either, which is just an area of caves, where (according to legend) the earliest men used to live in prehistoric times. Nothing but caves, where a few poor wretches eke out an existence – but that isn't what's called a village, at least not in Israel.

Capernaum, where my father Joseph had a house and workshop, which I inherited when he died.

Because I'm the eldest: four brothers who never accepted my sudden decision to lead a life of wandering, who have never followed me, who did everything they could to make me come back and live at home – and rightly so. And sisters who don't matter – for women don't much matter in Jewish society.

Four brothers, James, Joses, Judas and Simon. And a mother.

When people talk about me in the future, my father will just be an obscure figure, a patronymic attached to my name – *Jesus, son of Joseph*. There will also be a dearth of information about my mother – for what is there to say about a woman who has always behaved as a widow is expected to behave in Israel, who doesn't remarry and is obedient to the wishes of her eldest son, as she was to those of her late husband? As she has been to my younger brother James ever since I left the family home and ceased to be in charge of the workshop.

Ever since this life of wandering chose me, rather than me choosing it.

O Galilee of my childhood! A crossroads where all the peoples of the Orient constantly pass through, yet where Jewish farmers have stubbornly insisted on scratching out a living from the same plot of land for centuries, putting far more into it than they ever get in return. Within its wide, temperate horizons, the voice carries much farther than anywhere else. Being a craftsman and the son of a craftsman I have never worked the land, but it has provided me with many familiar images (as well as sounds and smells), all

of which nurture a child's inner life. Even when we were reasonably well off, due to the work we were doing during the rebuild-
ing of Sepphoris, the region's main city, I would still walk along
the road with the people bringing in the harvest, as well as the
grape-pickers on their way to the press and tenant farmers from
the nearby farms.

Someone who has never experienced a rural life such as ours,
cut off from Caesarea and Tiberias – idle, satin-clad cities – will
never be able to understand my parables or the impression they
made on the small farmers whom I grew up with. They were my
first audience, the only ones who were prepared to listen to what
I had to say. Every time I stood up to speak I made them mine, all
those faces craning towards me, with their wrinkles and a certain
look in their eye.

Not that they realized, but the words that seemed to flow from
my mouth actually came from them, from expectations of theirs
that are inseparable from the silence of the wilderness that has
dwelt within me ever since I was by the Jordan.

Which is why I rarely spoke to them about God. That's what
the Scribes and dignitaries from the Temple are for, they who are
always ready to pronounce the name of God. Along the byways
and on the hilltops, on the narrow plains of Galilee, the people
I met every day were similar to myself. No one has ever had to
prove the existence, the reality of God to them, because it was
engraved in the very fibre of their being. All that concerned them
was finding the path that led to him, the shortest and most reliable route.

They never took me for just another Greek philosopher, one of
the Cynics or Stoics who wander into our squares and marketplaces
and proceed to talk a lot of hot air. Nor one of our theologians,
who have so much to say on the subject of the Invisible. I had no
new beliefs to expound, only fleeting yet vivid glimpses of my own

experience, rooted as it is in that of the prophets of Israel, whether known or unknown.

I didn't try to teach them a different way of thinking: little by little I introduced them to my deep, personal relationship with the God of Moses.

3

In Capernaum, the farmers and fishermen rub shoulders without ever really getting to know each other. Greedy and grasping, inseparable from their nets, often working all night long, the men who fish the lake have little time for those who work the land and go to bed with the sun. I sometimes heard talk of people known as Zealots, fanatical nationalists who were "zealous for God". At the time they were regarded as common bandits, who were hunted down and taken to Jerusalem, where they were nailed onto crosses while still alive. In the Galilee of King Herod Antipas, my brothers and I were never aware that we were living under Roman occupation – my childhood was unremarkable, the days and seasons came and went in an atmosphere of unruffled tranquillity. At that age I probably came closest to what is usually described as simple happiness.

As in all Jewish families, the focal point of our lives was our mother. Everything we had came from her, everything led us back to her. She protected us from the worst of all the dangers that hang over a small Galilean village: a bad name. I was brought up not to attract attention, to be well regarded, never to become the subject of gossip – to be afraid of what people might say, of disapproving looks, pointed remarks. A Jewish mother is the custodian of her family's respectability, as well as, perhaps even more so, than its well-being, because worldly problems are generally only temporary, whereas a tarnished reputation stays with you to the grave.

My father Joseph was a devout Jew. It was his decision to take Nazirite vows, first for me and then for my brother James, which would encourage us to be pious later in life, to observe the purity laws. I stopped cutting my hair while I was still young; my flowing locks would be a reminder, both to me and to those around me, that I must never touch wine or lead a life of dissipation.

Overwhelmed by their sudden recovery, some of the people whose sufferings I eased proclaimed to all and sundry that I had learnt my art in Egypt, where my parents must have taken me soon after I was born. Unable to understand how the sickness had left their body, they insisted on regarding me as a sorcerer, like so many others in the region. I just let them say what they liked. Joseph make a journey to Egypt, when the farthest he had ever been was Sepphoris to the west and Jerusalem to the south? His horizons stretched no farther than his workshop, the village synagogue, his customers in the surrounding towns and our pilgrimages to the Temple – a narrowly circumscribed world, where I was expected to live out my life as well.

To carry on. To sink roots in the local community, like the cork oak trees that are embedded in the dry soil of the hills that slope gently down to the lake. To be known by everyone, greeted at every street corner as the respectable carpenter who can be relied upon to repair a roof or build a lean-to against the wall of a farmhouse. And also much in demand with his well-off customers, Jews and Romans alike, who by employing a small local craftsman can have villas built in Sepphoris or Tiberias at less expense. Respected come what may, because he was educated in the synagogue at Capernaum, the *Beth ha-sefer*, the House of the Book where the Pharisees hold sway.

To live a life as unruffled as the surface of the lake, whose unchanging calm ought to have been the backdrop to my existence.

Then came my meeting with John the Baptist, and the life that had been mapped out for me was shattered into a million pieces. Cutting me off from everyone, unexpectedly reintroducing me to myself.

The Pharisees... among the mists of childhood, they are the only memory that stands out. In our society, the eldest son receives a good education. Not required to work in the fields or mend fishing nets like most of the boys I was friends with, I spent far more time than they did in the cramped little room that led off the synagogue, where local rabbis handed down knowledge which left me in awe.

They taught Hebrew, a tongue similar to the Aramaic we use but which is rarely spoken. Although a dead language, it was essential if one was to read the Law, the mother and birth-giver of the Jewish people scattered throughout the Empire. "Wherever there is a Jew, there is the Law," our masters would drum into us. "And in whatever place Adonai gives him life, a Jew will find his homeland in the Law." I was privileged to have been born and to live in the Land of Israel, but only by diligently reading the Law would I become a real Jew. For my mother and father this justified all the sacrifices, the little gifts that were regularly given to the Pharisees, who were poorer than Job himself.

Their thinking was ruled by the memory of the great rabbi Hillel, who died twenty years ago. People say he studied in Jerusalem for forty years before going on to teach for another forty. A mild and gentle man, his interpretation of the Law was instilled into some of my teachers, who lived among the common people, while the strictness of his rival, Shammai, was much in vogue with the nationalists who were always stirring up trouble both in the towns and countryside. It is possible that Hillel's open-minded, tolerant approach, in which I was immersed from an early age, had a marked influence on my own teaching without my realizing it.

Day after day I studied the faded old scrolls of the Law, trying to fathom the regular-shaped letters by which I would gain access to the inner sanctum of Jewish identity.

Until the Sabbath day that no first-born son from a respectable family is able to avoid, when, in a packed synagogue, I stepped onto the dais facing the congregation. In the front row were the Pharisees, behind them the menfolk, and, in the shadows at the very back, the women, all wearing veils, among them my mother, who was bursting with pride. I took the gold-banded pen in my trembling hand, placed the tip on the first line of the scroll that lay open in front of me, and in my clear, high, child's voice I read one or two lines. My father, who knew the passage off by heart, was silently enunciating each and every word to himself, shaking with fright in case I made a mistake. When I looked up, he was so filled with emotion that he couldn't join in with the resounding *Amen* that made me a full member of God's Chosen People.

I remember the pilgrimages we used to make to the Temple for the Passover and the Feast of Tabernacles. Whichever direction you approach from, Jerusalem is the capital that you *go up* to with all your heart and soul. When we were met with the unforgettable sight of the city nestling round the Tower of David, surmounted – or rather crushed by the vast edifice that was still in the process of being built, we would stop for a moment. My father would put his prayer shawl on his head and we would sing the Psalms of Ascents, which had once brought hope to Jews in exile by the rivers of Babylon, helped renew their will to live.

For a simple country boy there was too much for my eyes and ears to take in all at once. In the shade beneath the columns that run along the esplanade of Solomon, the Scribes and Pharisees would converse all day long. Even had I dared go over to where they were gathered and listen to them, I wouldn't have understood a word of their pronouncements, they seemed to belong to a completely different race from the Pharisees in our village.

Unbeknown to me I was hearing the voices, catching glimpses of the faces of the very people who would eventually be responsible for me being where I am tonight. An outcast, hounded by the Jewish police for the words I have spoken, the people I have healed.

Hounded, and now finally within their clutches in the darkness of this lonely olive grove.

4

Reading the Law from a book is one thing, but understanding its boundless connotations is quite another. As ancient as the Jewish people itself, the Law can only give meaning and structure to our everyday lives if it is constantly adapted. This is the Pharisees' view and they act accordingly, unlike the Sadducees, those luminaries from Jerusalem for whom the Law is sufficient unto itself. They won't allow a single letter to be added to it, not even the smallest one in the Jewish alphabet, the yod. To them the Law is more than the image of God – it is a perfect reflection of him. Just as Adonai is immutable, the Law that proceeds from him is inviolable, the incarnation of Divine Majesty. It is the very presence of God among his people.

In contrast, the Pharisees spend every moment of their lives commenting on it. They maintain that by constantly moving forward they remain faithful to it, following the endless twists and turns of its complex argumentation, which they interpret using a strict set of rules. A single rabbi can challenge something that a whole succession of his forebears have already laid down, as long as he refers to the teachings that have gone before. Only build on what exists already. Add a stone, yes, but beware of digging the foundations of a new house in virgin soil, however humble it may be.

Like all living things, the Law grows day by day – but it never gets any older. The Pharisees seek to help a single, unique being, born long ago from the mouth of God himself while bolts of lightning flashed round Mount Sinai, to develop and mature. We are born only once: to grow is to be yourself, while becoming someone else.

To the Ten Commandments they added 613 precepts that provide a framework for every moment of a Jew's life. My teachers, almost feverish with elation, or perhaps just out of breath, appeared to regard this number as fixed. Their every effort was dedicated to categorizing them, putting them in order of priority from the most to the least important, from the first to the last. In the Law, nothing is unimportant: for them, arranging the different levels in the pyramid of precepts is to establish order in the world and then to live by it.

It was in this way that I learnt how to reason using a method which no other nation, no civilization apart from ours has ever been able to master. Respect for ancient traditions goes hand in hand with respect for the person with whom one is speaking. When he asks a question – which inevitably undermines the foundations of an edifice that is perfect by its very nature – it would be wrong to reply in a way which brings the discussion to a close, preventing the Law, as well as the other person, from developing. For a Pharisee, to live is constantly to challenge. To conclude the debate with an imperious assertion would be to obstruct a vital process.

One question must always be answered with another. Greek and Roman philosophers try to throw their opponent off balance with the weight of their argument, to close the gap that has been opened up by his enquiries. The local Pharisees taught me to redress the balance by responding in kind: hence the questions meet each other halfway, and the answer appears of its own accord, clear and irrefutable, a ray of divine light illuminating the darkness of the human mind.

Because of this process of argumentation, every Pharisee remains in constant conflict with all his fellows. Yet this doesn't exclude any of them from the life-giving waters of the Law, that endless stream which irrigates our people, enriches them. Thanks to this, despite being small and insignificant, this people is alive – and will go on living for ever.

Israel's state of ceaseless and obligatory debate must always take place in public view. In a shady alleyway, in the village marketplace as much as under Solomon's Gate, a discussion between two Jews about a point of the Law immediately draws a crowd of eager listeners who are aware that their presence represents the people as a whole, elected once and for all time. Thanks to them, Israel never stops questioning itself. At any time of the day or night, any rabbi, whether he is the great Hillel himself or a humble man who teaches in a synagogue somewhere in Upper Galilee, can be stopped in the street by any Jew. Never does he regard this as a nuisance or an imposition: setting aside whatever he is doing, he addresses himself to the question at hand, and together he and the other person, be he king or beggar, open the floodgates of the Law.

By allowing me to see them constantly engaged in it, the Pharisees in Capernaum taught me the solemn and subtle art of dispute. People say I am a past master at it. This was one of the reasons I became famous; it might also have been the cause of my downfall.

5

My father's passing left not a trace, either in our village or my memory. One more Jew had departed from Eretz Israel having fulfilled his task of bringing sons into the world and teaching them to respect our traditions. I fasted on the appointed days, always carried out the ritual ablutions after going to the market, never ate without first purifying my hands, while the fragrant dish which my mother put on the table at every mealtime had first been meticulously washed inside and out by her personally. In this way nothing I put in my mouth could make me impure.

This scrupulous observance of the purity laws wasn't at all unusual; it was expected from a man who had assumed the mantle of Nazirite vows, more so than an ordinary Jew. They are undemanding rules, which allow us to retain our identity when living among Gentiles, where there is always a danger that our race might die out.

These rules were taken to extremes, in a sense blown out of proportion by the Essenes whom I sometimes came across. Not the ones who live in closed communities north of the oasis at Ein Feshkha, on the barren shores of the Dead Sea, who choose to cut themselves off from the common run of humanity due to their bleak view of the world, which inspires the rest of us with a blend of admiration and disgust. With them, the requirements of ritual purity, which are regarded by ordinary Jews as beneficial, have been taken to such extremes that they seem beyond the capabilities of any human being; neither the Law nor the precepts require such severity. And if they advocate hatred for those who aren't part of their group, it is probably because they are unable to love themselves. Witnessing their lack of moderation would help me develop the twofold commandment to love, which springs as naturally from the Law as it does from my own experience of God.

But the Essenes whom I occasionally met were the ones who live in most towns and villages, and have jobs and families like the rest of us. The only thing that tends to set them apart is that they use a slightly different calendar to ours, and their unusually formal custom of scrupulously washing before meals. And, of course, they reject the form of worship used in the Temple in Jerusalem.

Yet a growing number of Jews could no longer tolerate the outrageous sight of business being conducted within the Temple precincts: the grasping moneylenders, the price that had to be paid to procure God's forgiveness by sacrificing an animal, the size and weight of which is designed above all to broadcast the wealth of the wealthy and the poverty of the poor. Because they declare themselves to be the purest of the pure, and staunchly refuse to make any concessions to that despised class, the higher clergy, the populace are well disposed towards the Essenes, a view I shared for a long time without really reflecting on it.

It never occurred to me to join one of their desert communities, unlike some people I have never even been one to abide by their rules as part of everyday life. In any case, for me the question never arose: among the various yet distinct factions that exist within my native religion, it is the Pharisees for whom I felt the most natural affinity. They are the ones who educated me, trained me in their intellectual rigour, taught me everything I know. So eventually, by which time I had grown a short beard, I donned one of the robes they wear, edged with a fringe.

On that day the child of the synagogue, the orphan with a family to look after, the respected craftsman whose services everyone needed, the ordinary young Jew from an ordinary Galilean village became one of those small, nameless Pharisees who travel round the countryside and the shores of the lake, passing on their love of the Law and the custom of contemplating it without ceasing.

From that day on, everyone referred to me informally as Rabbi.

6

There now began the most anonymous period of my life, no longer lit by childhood grace, nor as yet by any sense of a calling.

My brothers helped me in the workshop, but it was I who dealt with the clients. Some of them, especially those from Sepphoris, were clearly from a higher social class than me. These Hellenized Jews were very different from the ordinary people with whom I always felt comfortable and whose language I spoke. It wasn't only the use of Greek, and the pride they took in using it, in which the barriers between us manifested themselves. They were from a different world, one to which the prospect of hard times was unknown, having avoided the difficulties faced by other Jews, first by becoming assimilated with the occupying forces and then their values.

Yet is it really possible to talk of values, whether moral or spiritual? A sense of being master of all they survey, as well as the arrogance that comes from having a high opinion of oneself seems, for these social climbers, to have made unnecessary the disquiet that results from the constant questioning which gives structure to a Jew's inner life. Blinded by the glittering prizes of wealth and power, the members of this elite behave disdainfully towards their fellow countrymen, who are still bound by the Law, and who as far as they are concerned don't exist. The Zealots, who are constantly plotting to wipe them off the face of the earth, no longer regard them as patriots. While for the vast majority of people, who stand aside to let them pass by in their litters with the curtains closed, they are Jews only in name. Most of them collaborate quite overtly with the occupiers, collecting the taxes that burden us or running private estates belonging to wealthy landowners.

Had I not been a small businessman, nothing would have brought me into contact with these people. Is it my provincial upbringing, which sets store by observing proprieties and good manners, or that I felt duty-bound to do so for commercial reasons? Outside our business relationship, I struck up friendships with some of these individuals who lived in a different world to mine, and who supported me materially when I began to travel around preaching. In their company I lost that reticence which simple people tend to show towards those from higher up the social scale, either out of shyness or to be ingratiating. I even lost much of my self-consciousness, which would later help me feel as much at ease with influential people as with ordinary working folk. These acquaintances of mine dazzled my companions, who thanks to me were invited to feasts where they stuffed themselves with food and drink the like of which they had never seen in their lives – which earned me a reputation, quite unfairly, as a glutton and a winebibber.

I also managed to acquire a basic knowledge of Greek, which enabled me to make myself more or less understood to a Roman centurion whom I met somewhere on the road, as well as a Syrian woman whom I came across on the other side of our northern border.

Because of the tricks played by my memory, I am now unable to see a direct connection between this admittedly long period of my life and the abrupt change of heart that might have led me here, to the night of my arrest.

At the time, none of the directions I took seemed to lead any-where. My self-knowledge was still hazy and ill defined, often as a result of a stereotypically Jewish way of life. I had already exceeded the age for starting a family as laid down by the Pharisees – every Jewish male knows that he was born incomplete, and that only by a union of the flesh with a woman can he achieve union with himself, with other people and with God.

Women were never a matter of indifference to me, and I could see quite clearly that they weren't just looking at me: they felt drawn to me, something that would eventually grow into the incredible devotion that some of them showed towards me. Erotic love, elevated by the Greeks and Romans to the level of the divine, is for the Jew simply a reflection – although the most meaningful of all – of what his relationship with God will be at the end of time. A synthesis of one into the other, without commingling yet with-out impediment, a total communion that words cannot express, a happiness that to our bodies is inevitably fleeting yet which is never-ending. Inspired by the Psalms and the Song of Solomon, our most well-known rabbis speak without reservation about this sexual union, which they hold up as an example to young people and a duty for adults.

But the years went by and still I didn't marry. Of course, a vol-untary and lifelong state of celibacy isn't unknown among our people – although rare, it has always been both the concomitant and the crowning glory of the prophetic calling. Or occasionally – and equally rarely – a deliberate choice made by members of extremist sects, such as the desert Essenes. Yet I wasn't an Essene. Nor at that stage did I sense any calling to follow in the footsteps of Elijah and the prophets who came after him.

Because she had to defer to me as head of the family, my mother never dared put the question which she must have been dying to ask: "When are you going to ask me to choose a nice young girl with whom you will fulfil the obligation of every Jewish man, and start a family?"

As for my brothers, they were already riddled with the jealousy that would eventually burst out when I set off on my life of wandering. The fact that they never spoke when I was present was a symptom of the same lack of understanding from which I was to suffer so much later on. James, who like me was a Nazirite, would wear out his knees making prostrations every time we went on a pilgrimage to the Temple. These formal devotions, which even then were not my way, have probably made him blind – or indifferent – to what fate held for his elder brother.

With those around me rarely speaking to me, and my Pharisee friends preoccupied with their endless disputes, the fact that I was still a bachelor ceased to be an issue. Perhaps people thought I was delaying getting married until I was older, because of my family responsibilities? After all, that was for me to decide.

So why, and as a matter of urgency, didn't I ask myself this same question, which is at once intensely private and of public interest (a Jew without issue betrays his people)?

I don't know. Perhaps – although it's only now that this occurs to me – I was already tormented by the sense of disquiet that would eventually drive me into the wilderness?

Neither the constant antipathy expressed by the nationalists towards the Romans and the Jewish aristocracy, nor the loathing I shared with them and many other people for the form of worship used in the Temple, nor the cloud that hangs permanently over the esplanade of Solomon, that stench of burnt animal fat which catches you in the throat as soon as you walk through the Sheep Gate, nor the discontent at the woeful state of decay in Jewish society, nothing could justify suddenly severing my ties with a way of life that was as firmly established as the statues in the Roman

32

amphitheatre in Jerusalem, which no Jew could bear to look at because it reminded him of the act of sacrilege that their presence represented.

Nothing, except the voice of one man.

A voice that rang out all over Israel, even beyond its borders.

The voice of John the Baptist, the prophet of the Jordan.

7

It is many years since the voice of the prophets has been heard in Israel. The prophetic tradition, which acts as a necessary counterbalance to the all-pervading Law, has always provided an unconventional way into the Invisible. But nowadays the prophets are merely great men from the past, authorities to whom we are expected to defer. Yet a nation cannot survive on its past alone: the goad that kept us going for so many years is no longer there. In its stead are the beginnings of a radical apocalyptic movement, moralizers who predict the end of the world and mesmerize people, strike terror into their hearts.

For several years, one of these voices had come from the Judaean desert. Its fiery breath reached as far as the remotest towns and villages, like the dust storms that whip up in the rocky, wide-open expanses before blowing themselves out in our farmyards. The power of it drew Jews from all directions and backgrounds.

Little was known about John the Baptist. Was he from a priestly family? Or had he been brought up from an early age by the Essenes at Qumran, trained in the strict discipline of the Baptist ways? Yet unlike them he only baptized a person once, after a process of inner conversion of which immersion in the River Jordan was the outward sign. His unconcealed opposition to the moral standards of Herod and his court made him immensely popular with the ordinary people, who were appalled that the son of an Idumean should be sitting on a throne that he sullied by committing incest.

Attracted, as were so many others, by his charisma, I used a journey to the south as an excuse to go to Bethany-beyond-the-Jordan, where John was baptizing. The fact that I didn't tell anyone where I was going shows how uncertain I was in my mind at the time, unwittingly prey to that typically Jewish disquiet, although the extent of its hold over me was something I refused to admit to myself.

So eventually, among a crowd of many different people, I went to hear this voice.

Close to its mouth on the Dead Sea, the Jordan flowed through the surrounding sand dunes. Standing in bright sunlight in the deep part of the river, a man was leaning forward, taking those who came to him and plunging them under the living water one by one. Sometimes he stood up, and harangued the crowd of spellbound onlookers:

"You brood of vipers! Who warned you to flee from the wrath to come? Even now the axe is lying at the root of the trees; every tree therefore that does not bear good fruit is cut down and thrown into the fire!"

What I saw was a man ranting and raving, declaring that the world was about to sink into a fiery furnace; the hurricane was almost upon us, an apocalypse that would uproot everything – even Israel, who thought she was protected by her Covenant with God. A false sense of security! A terrible judgement was about to sweep down upon us, the end of the world was nigh and no one would be spared.

Dazzled by this fervent flame that was reflected in the surface of the flowing water, I looked round at the crowd. There were artisans, small farmers, fisherman who could be recognized by the patched smocks that barely covered their emaciated bodies. Among them were plump men with glowing complexions, a few Pharisees from Jerusalem identifiable by the long fringes on their robes, Sadducees proudly wearing their traditional tall hats. Guards from the Temple, who looked astonished to find themselves in such a place, and who were no doubt sent to protect all these dignitaries – who if they hadn't been here would never have had a chance to rub shoulders with the populace and inhale their smells.

Everyone appeared to be terrified by this prophet of doom, and from the water there came a chorus of groans: "What then should we do to escape the coming wrath?" Since the day of doom was unavoidable, said John, they should try and escape the worst of it: they must *be converted*, stop stealing, ill-treating people, extorting money. In a word, share all they had with the poor.

John the Baptist's grim, ominous tone made a deep and lasting impression on me. Once I got home and reimmersed myself in the humdrum routine of the workshop, the voice I had heard by the Jordan kept on echoing in my mind incessantly. I knew that my life had changed for ever. John had held up the blazing inferno of the apocalypse before my eyes; dazzled by it, everything about the life I had led up till then suddenly struck me as prosaic, occupations and people alike. On the shores of the lake nothing had changed, yet to me it was now flat and colourless. This world of ours was doomed, the end was upon us: the axe had *already* fallen on the tree of Israel.

I began going to the synagogue outside of normal services more often. I would unroll the scroll containing the books of the prophets and come across passages in Isaiah such as this: "Every valley shall be filled, and every mountain and hill shall be made low, and the crooked shall be made straight, and the rough ways made smooth." So was this the *conversion* that the Baptist had spoken of? It also said: "Prepare the way of the Lord." Was John claiming that he had cleared the debris that had blocked the path for years, all the detritus left behind by Israel's slow, inevitable decline? Imprisoned within the walls of their all-too-subtle reasoning, weren't the Pharisees who had taught me just going round in circles in a locked room to which they didn't have the key? How could we escape the wrath to come?

All of a sudden my life seemed insipid, restricted, shrivelled up. If there was a vital thread, a way that would give meaning to the different things I had done, I was now certain – although I couldn't explain why – that it would appear as a result of answering John the Baptist's call. Perhaps he was now Elijah's heir? Through him, on the banks of the Jordan, would there be the long-awaited revival of the prophetic tradition which we had lost hope of ever seeing? I simply *had* to go to this window that had opened on the edge of the wilderness.

It was quite normal for a devout Jew, particularly a Nazirite, to spend some time with a spiritual father, to sit at the feet of a well-known rabbi or one of the hermits in the desert – such as Bannus, who not long after John the Baptist led a life similar to his. I told my mother and my brothers that I was going to be away for a few weeks; James would be in charge of the workshop in my absence. I made no attempt to hide, either from them or my friends, the fact that I was going to see the hermit on the Jordan. They were pleased at the decision, which would only increase my standing as a young Pharisee. My colleagues had already asked me to read from the Law in the synagogue in Capernaum on the Sabbath. Once I got back, they suggested I might also like to give a homily, the official commentary that follows the reading. Filled with pride at the prospect of seeing her eldest son formally established as a rabbi, it was with a gratified expression that my mother watched me set off.

Exhausted by the walk, I dropped my bundle of belongings at the top of a sand dune and sat down. On the riverbank and in the deepest part of the water, towards which people were thronging to be cleansed of their sins, nothing had changed. How far away the Temple and its atoning sacrifices seemed! There was no blood here, no fatty burnt offerings on the sacrificial altar; just people going down to the bank, bowing to the Baptist who then submerged them in the river.

I didn't realize that it was at this moment that my life would take a completely different turn, and one that would be permanent. Or that by some inexorable process, the path on which I was about to set foot would lead me to this empty garden on a moonlit paschal night.

As alone here as I was in the wilderness.

8

I found that there were three different types of people who con-
verged on John the Baptist.

There were those who came to see the performance, usually
from Jerusalem. According to John, his baptism was both the end
result and the completion of the journey of *conversion* of which he
spoke, by which those who were baptized would escape the flames.
But as far as anyone could see, plunging converts into the water
didn't seem to bring about any outward change. They resurfaced
with water streaming off them, and then walked away, to all ap-
pearances no different, and were then followed by others. What
was there to show that they weren't the same as before? That they
had experienced an inner conversion? By the time evening came
these onlookers decided there wasn't anything worth seeing, so
they left, with a faint feeling of unease that only lasted for as long
as it took to return to their everyday lives.

Others settled themselves in the huts made of branches that had
sprung up everywhere on the dunes, some way from the riverbank.

Still others had pitched camp permanently near to where John
was baptizing. More than well-wishers, these were the Baptist's
most fervent supporters, in some cases of long standing, in fact
(or so they said) for life. With a certain pretentiousness, surprising

41

for such uncultured men, they referred to themselves as *Talmîdā* –
the Aramaic translation of the Greek word *mathètès,* a name that
pagan philosophers give to their disciples, and which is foreign to
Judaism.

I wasn't one of the Baptist's disciples, and I wasn't intending to
stay longer than a few days. One of the huts made of branches was
empty, so I made myself at home, strengthened the roof, then lit
a fire in the middle of three stones. After that I went and sat on a
sand dune, isolated from John by a small crowd that had gathered
on the slope below.

It was some time before I dared to bridge this gap, which was
a sign of my lack of self-knowledge. Come evening, I finally felt
able to go and sit by the fire, where, now most of the crowd had
left, John was eating locusts that he had toasted and dipped in
wild honey. Despite his rough, unsociable manner we soon struck
up an understanding.

He probed me for information about myself. I gave brief answers.
His questions were like a surgical blade, slicing through the suture-
like reticence that kept my lips tightly sealed. He seemed to go
deeper than I or anyone else had gone before – except perhaps God.

Then he stopped talking. And in the dancing firelight, his silence
was like another voice.

I have always been unforthcoming, or at least that's what people
used to say about me in Capernaum. Yet when I encountered John's
silence, I realized that thoughts, ideas, the fruitless answers to my
questions were fluttering around inside my head like a constantly
twittering bird in a cage created by my reticence. Thoughts scrolled
past one after another in an endless stream, transforming my outward silence into a great clamouring inside me.

As I opened my heart to the Baptist, he stopped poking the fire
and looked at me for a long time. From that moment on he was

glad to find an opportunity for us to talk privately now and then, to the amazement of his disciples, who were furious to see such a close rapport growing between their master and myself, something they longed for but could never hope to achieve.

So what exactly did he say? All I can remember is his deep voice. But when I left him and went back to my hut, where I lay staring up through the branches of the roof, watching stars race across the endless night sky, I was suddenly seized with a burning desire for the wilderness.

Only if you are utterly naked will you find what you seek. A whole nation comes here to bathe and cleanse itself. But you need more, you need the crucible that will melt the fat from your soul. From me you have heard the call and a promise: the wilderness will carve out the inner man, turn you into someone else and yet the same person. Go out into the wilderness, then come and see me again. For then you will understand. I think these are the words he used, this man who seemed to have seen deeper into my soul than I had.

"*I recall your youthful grace when you went out to me in an unfertile land,*" is what God once said to one of the prophets. Forgetting Capernaum, the sound of the water lapping on the shores of the lake, my mother and my brothers, unable to resist the call of the wilderness, I left my belongings beside the fire in my hut, which by now had gone out. To avoid being seen, at dawn I set off along the stony path that runs along the western side of the Dead Sea.

When the sun came up, before it kissed the deep, still waters of the Dead Sea, it washed an ochre tint across the vast expanse that stretched away to my right: the Judaean desert in all its bleakness.

It was the very reflection of what I saw in myself. Now I was going to have to cultivate this infertile land.

9

I kept walking until I saw the green smudge of an oasis in the distance. The Essenes from Qumran have settled in the north, in an area of level, arid ground in the shadow of tall cliffs. I sat in the mouth of a cave and waited.

Walking past below I saw a member of the sect, identifiable by his brilliant white smock. He looked up at me, and then he was gone.

That evening, another man in white came to speak to me. No one can survive on his own in the desert, he said. You seek the solitude that cleanses? This is where you will find it. Behind you lies utter destitution. Travel far into its depths, far enough to forget about us but not too far, so you can come and drink regularly from our springs. Sometimes you will find a few dates on this rock. They will help keep you alive without breaking your fast. You are not one of us, but simply being here proves that you are a man after our own heart.

The next minute he was gone.

I travelled far, far out across this anvil upon which the sun beat down constantly like a hammer. When all I could see was a vastness that was indistinguishable from the sky, I stopped. There was a rocky outcrop, which, although not offering complete shade, provided enough cover for me to survive. I settled down at the base, where it seemed to grow from the ground: something else was going to grow here too.

If needs be I would wait for forty days, like the Prophet Elijah.

Minute by minute, a mere frail bundle of humanity lost between the sand and the sky, I pushed my body to breaking point. If time were to pass slowly, all that would be left to me was the light gradually following its course round the sky, until night fell and it faded to deep blue. I wanted to listen, to let a voice well up inside me. The words it speaks are not those of men. I shall try to hear what lies beyond the words, the words I learnt to say as a devout Jewish boy.

John the Baptist had created a longing in me that could only be satisfied by silence.

I would wait.

The silence of the wilderness is deafening; not a bird flying past, not even one of the crickets whose shrill chirruping makes the nights in Galilee so bewitching. Perhaps I would have to go beyond the silence, or perhaps, once it ceased to be something outside of me, when it had filled me to my depths, I would no longer be able to hear it.

The one I am waiting for is in that silence, yet he is beyond it.

At night, stretched out on the ground staring up at the sky, I heard the song of the stars. And I realized that it was the origin of the prophets' words, bearing witness to the existence of the One God of Israel. They rocked me to sleep with their cradle-like glow.

I untied the plaits worn by Nazirites and let my hair hang loose over my shoulders. The breeze would sometimes blow it across my face; whenever I didn't unconsciously brush it back, I knew the silence wasn't far away.

And then strange apparitions started surging up inside my head. Let loose by the lack of thoughts, a fearsome opponent was attacking me, harrying me until my inner life began to ebb away. I knew it was *the Evil One*, whom Israel traditionally portrays as *Satan* or *the Devil*, he who divides. He danced round and round inside me, as if mocking me in that ironic, fiendish way of his, knowing that I was in his clutches, that my attempt to escape was just the result of my pride.

All men are made to serve me – this is what he whispered in my ear. Wealth, power, worldly delights in all their different forms are what I use to enslave you. Neither God nor his angels can loose your chains, for I too am one of God's creatures.

I faced up to him with all my might and cried out:

"Get thee behind me, Satan!"

Eventually, exhausted by the struggle, I wept. The tears that trickled down my weather-beaten cheeks gave me life, even more than the springs I dragged myself to every evening in order to drink.

I will never be able to describe the days and nights that came in the wake of those tears, for they have been wiped from my mind, leaving only the memory of a vortex of pain. I thought I was going to die, and in fact I did. The death I died in the crucible of the desert cannot be put in words, or compared with anything experienced by mankind. The wilderness – that magnificent landscape whose praises Jewish and Arab poets have sung through the ages – was no longer around me: it had now filled me to my depths, a place at once shimmering and filled with desolation.

But I survived these diabolical attacks. They didn't help me grow, yet nor did they destroy me. I knew that from now on the Enemy would be at my side day and night, that I would find him in every person I met, that he would do everything in his power to control my thoughts, my urges, my every human feeling. Even when the time came for me to die a second time, I would still have to face him, choose between him and the God of silence.

So I shall live with you. But no longer will you frighten me, because I know what lies behind your mask.

Without hearing voices, not even deep inside me, I had discovered a hidden side to God, a face concealed by the heavy mantle of the traditions I had grown up with. I now had a better understanding of what John the Baptist taught, but I no longer shared his bleak outlook. It is true that this world is dead: yet it isn't doomed to disappear in some fearful apocalypse, it will live on. God doesn't judge with fire alone.

This intuition would guide me throughout my whole life.

John the Baptist was right. When I headed back into the north, to people whose human qualities never live up to our expectations, I was still Jesus the son of Joseph, the young Pharisee from Galilee. But I was no longer the same person.

The wilderness had lit a raging fire inside me, which would never stop burning until it had totally consumed me.

When I went past Qumran, I didn't stop off to take leave of the Essenes, whose friendly presence had helped me survive in the vast stony expanse. There was now a tenuous bond between us, one that I would never completely dismiss.

10

After the shadows of the ravine hemmed in by red and grey rocks, the bright sunlight came as a shock. About a mile away was a thin strip of greenery – the Jordan. Beyond it was more desert, while the distant hills of Perea in Transjordan were silhouetted against the horizon.

Screwing up my eyes, I could just make out what I was looking for. In the heat haze, barely distinguishable from the sparse bushes on the banks, dark smudges were moving back and forth, a mass of activity gravitating round a central point which I wasn't yet able to see: John the Baptist.

Staggering slightly, I made my way over to the familiar dunes. The usual crowd of people, who were drawn irresistibly to the water, moved aside as I stumbled down the slope. They all stared at me in amazement – at my long hair plastered with sand, my cracked, sunburnt skin, the inner fire whose blaze must have been clearly visible without me realizing…

John had just baptized someone; all I could see was the skin and bone of his shoulders. He turned round slowly and just stood staring at me, not moving. It was up to me to take the final step and go to him, become a disciple.

I walked into the water, which coursed between my legs. As if rooted to the spot, he stared into my eyes and mumbled: "I need to be baptized by you, and do you come to me?..."

So he understood. If I agreed to be one of his disciples, it would be in order to leave him. To venture into places where he had never been able to go. Without answering I leant towards the water, and John pressed gently on my head and shoulders.

I spent the rest of the day alone, sitting on a sand dune some way off. Occasionally a gust of wind would bring snatches of what John was saying:

"Among you," he told the crowd, "stands one whom you do not know..."

It was me he was talking about, and he was right: no one knew me here, I didn't even know myself any more. There was a potent force welling up inside me, like a boil about to burst – and yet I hadn't changed. I would have to wait till the boil came to a head, but I didn't belong here any more.

So where did I belong in Israel now?

All Jews are born into a state of disquiet; yet since I returned from the melting pot of the wilderness I had stopped feeling the same sense of disquiet as these Jews. I sensed convictions growing in me, although what these were was still unclear. Before I could give voice to them, I would have to wait and see where events would lead me.

The next day I paced to and fro on the top of the dunes, trying to decide what to do. Down by the river, John was talking to some of his disciples. Looking up, he saw my figure and pointed to me. I didn't want to talk to him or anyone else at that moment, so I turned away and headed slowly towards my hut.

I hadn't gone far when I heard footsteps crunching on the sand behind me and turned round. Two men were following me, one behind the other, not daring to approach me. After a moment's hesitation I shouted to them rather brusquely:

"What are you looking for?"

The one in front stepped aside for his companion, who answered nervously:

"Rabbi, where are you staying?"

With his lilting voice, gnarled muscles and patched smock he was clearly from Galilee, perhaps one of the men who fished the lake. And he had called me Rabbi – so he knew who I was, or rather, who I *used* to be. The other man stood behind him, slightly older and with an undemonstrative, elegant air about him. Like mine his coat was made from a single piece of cloth: so he was from the city, and didn't say a word. No more welcoming than before, I replied:

"Come and see."

It was about the tenth hour, two hours before sunset.

They spent the evening with me around the tiny little fire, which cast its light across our faces. Andrew – that was what the Galilean was called – talked and asked questions. As I had thought, the other man was from Jerusalem – a Judaean who didn't give his name, and I didn't ask. In no particular order I told them about how dissatisfied I was with life by the lake, how I had met John the Baptist, the time I had spent in the wilderness. I wasn't able to describe my experiences there, because it still wasn't clear in my own mind. The Judaean didn't speak, he just listened. All evening I could feel his eyes boring into me, as if he were lost in thought, turning things over in his mind. And immediately I felt closer to him than to his garrulous and rather boorish companion.

Andrew hadn't come all the way to the Jordan by himself – his brother and two other Galileans were with him. All four regarded themselves as John's disciples, and when I looked enquiringly at the Judaean he nodded: he too had been baptized. The only thing that these unrefined individuals seemed to have in common – albeit superficially – with this well-bred town-dweller was that all five belonged to the movement embodied by the hermit of the Jordan.

The next day I decided to go home. In the morning, Andrew introduced me to his brother Simon, known as the *Barjona*.

What a coarse face he had, such a curt manner, and that combative way of drawing attention to his nickname, which suited him so well! In our native Aramaic *barjona* means "barren, empty, desolate", and by extension "outside the law, in exile". Among other names it was one used by the brigands who terrorized the local population, and who would later become the Zealots with whom I came into conflict. I heard that like many other young Galileans, Simon had lived among them for a while, shared their life of adventure before going back to his nets. When he joined me, bringing his rough and unsubtle ways to our band of wanderers, I stopped using his nickname, which was far too apt, and called him Peter instead.

Without further ado, Andrew and Peter brought Philip to see me, who like them lived in the little lakeside port of Bethsaida. At about midday, Philip fetched their fourth confederate, Nathanael, who was from Cana, a village some distance inland. He was a rabbinical student whose dream was to become a Scribe, in other words to specialize in the Law. Like them he was seized with the fanatical conviction that the Kingdom of David would shortly be restored. The first time we met I had to impress on him that I wasn't party to this political and religious frenzy. Would they like to accompany me on my journey back to Galilee? Very well – as long as it was clear that I didn't share their extremist longings. I foresaw something quite different, something that had come to me in the wilderness, but I didn't go into detail: it wasn't yet time for that.

That evening we set off northwards. Peter, Andrew, Philip, Natha-nael – and the Judaean, who suddenly decided to come with us at the last minute, although he didn't say why. The others weren't particularly keen on his company, they just seemed to put up with it without really accepting him.

Before leaving the Jordan I walked up onto the dunes. Below me, John the Baptist was just sending away the last of the day's pilgrims. I stayed where I was, silhouetted against the sky, until our eyes met. In his there was a look of great world-weariness, but also what might have been a fleeting glint of joy.

Meeting this man had been a turning point in my life. I would never see him again.

11

Once past the oasis at Jericho, the most direct route is through Samaria. Nathanael was keen to put in an appearance in Cana, the village where he was born, where there was due to be a wedding, one of those Jewish celebrations that goes on for a week and to which the whole district is invited. He told me that my mother and brothers were sure to be there. I could meet up with them, and after the festivities we could all travel back to Capernaum together.

So we travelled through the land of the Samaritans, heretics whom the Jews were so anxious to avoid that they would take a long, roundabout route via Transjordan in order to bypass their territory. We spent the night at the foot of Mount Gerizim. At the top stood their temple, which they regarded as the only one in which it was fitting to speak to God, and where they used a form of worship quite different from the rite practised in Jerusalem.

The Temple of Jerusalem, the Temple of Gerizim! I didn't join in with my companions' scathing remarks about their respective qualities. Ever since I had gazed at the stars in the wilderness I had been convinced that if there was a place where we could meet God, it wasn't to be found in any temple, or indeed in any specific spot.

I was unaware that one of the inner boundaries I was about to cross was the very one that divides Jews from Samaritans.

During the three-day journey I said little. Striding along at the front, the four Galileans filled the air with words, to which I paid little attention. Like me, the Judaean rarely spoke. Unaccustomed to the odd sound of our Aramaic, perhaps he was reluctant to take part in the conversation. And also like me, he could probably sense that they instinctively mistrusted him. He walked beside me, letting them go on ahead; I valued his silence, which showed thoughtfulness, and was already evidence of a respectful attitude.

During our visit to the festivities in Cana, only one otherwise unremarkable incident stood out. As it happened, my mother and brothers were there, among a large and fairly intoxicated crowd. Because my hair was still hanging over my shoulders, everyone understood why I didn't help myself to the wine that was being constantly brought round. The week-long celebrations were drawing to a close; vast quantities of food and drink must have been consumed by the guests over the past few days. I kept quiet and stayed in the background, looking forward to getting home.

Then I felt my mother's gentle touch on my arm.

"They have no more wine," she whispered in my ear.

As sober as I was myself, she was the only one to have realized there was a domestic problem that the chief steward (who was very drunk) would have been unable to solve even if he had been in a fit state to notice. Foreseeing a disaster – a wedding reception suddenly running out of wine, bringing disgrace on the bridegroom – she had come to tell the head of her own family, as was usual.

I replied curtly: "Woman, what concern is that to you and to me?" – a brusqueness that was as overt as it was customary: it is out of the question for a Jewish man to be friendly towards a woman in public, even his own mother. She had a quiet word with the servants, who took me to an alcove where there were six large water jars that were being kept cool. Looking inside, I saw they contained that bitter and quite undrinkable syrup which in hot climates like ours is used for making wine. It had to be diluted in just the right proportions to turn it into a drink fit for the gods.

I glanced over at the steward, who, his face very flushed, was holding forth with gusto in the main room. I had often seen this delicate operation performed at my wealthy customers' houses, transforming concentrated extract into wine suitable for drinking. I beckoned to the servants: one by one they filled the jars with fresh water, waiting for me to give them the sign to stop pouring.

When they took a cup to the chief steward, he was amazed at how good the wine was: in the middle of the festivities, who was still clear-headed enough to get the subtle mixture exactly right?

But by then I was already rounding up my brothers and the four Galileans – they had had enough to eat and drink; it was time to go.

On the way out I bumped into the Judaean. Also sober, he had seen everything, and the smile he gave me was a sign that this little incident had strengthened the understanding between us. So I wasn't just a country carpenter – I was familiar with the ways of his world! He was going back to Jerusalem and his household, who were expecting him. As he said goodbye, he told me that the very next time I was there, he would be sure to see me.

The sun was low in the sky when I saw the perfect oval of the lake, breathed in its deliciously damp, fresh air.

Deep down inside me, the molten lava that had built up during my time of testing in the wilderness was still simmering away. If it were ever to burst out, consuming all that lay in its path, then it would be here, in this landscape that seemed to be meant for nothing more than the happiness of a peaceful existence.

12

So as not to transgress the law of the Sabbath, we arrived in Capernaum on Friday evening, just before sunset. The next day I went to the synagogue where I had gone as a boy, as was my custom. Everyone I saw greeted the young rabbi whom they had watched grow up, and who in their eyes would be for ever wreathed with the esteem that came from having spent time with the ascetic of the Jordan. They knew, and would never know any more than that. There are inner rifts that words cannot describe.

After the chanting of the *Shemoneh Esrei*, the eighteen Ritual Blessings that lay the world at the feet of even the least significant Jew, I was handed the scroll. I saw that it was open at the Book of Isaiah, a verse that I had always found particularly moving, and which had prompted me to go to John the Baptist: "The spirit of the Lord God is upon me…"

I must have read in a distinctive way, because the congregation suddenly started to pay special attention. In the front row, the *hazzan* – the chief cantor who led the congregation in prayer – nodded at me: for the first time I was allowed to continue, and give the official commentary on the passage.

Fire of the wilderness, tide of lava within me, held back until now by my silence, convictions won at a high price, mysterious

Awakening which leads who knows where... Was this the right moment?

Yet the decision wasn't mine to take – the words just came of their own accord, heedless and uncontainable:

"Today this scripture has been fulfilled in your hearing..."

Ignoring the suddenly set expressions on people's faces, I continued. The Pharisaical commentary on the Law is intended to show how it can and should be fulfilled in a gradual way in the course of our everyday lives. But this wasn't what I was saying. I was declaring to all those present that the Law *had been fulfilled* at this very moment, in this very place – that is to say, by me. On hearing this assertion, which they would immediately start considering from every possible angle, assessing its potential and unprecedented ramifications, my fellow Pharisees instinctively pricked up their ears. For if the Law was fulfilled – if it had nothing more to achieve – then their entire lives, which were wholly devoted to a never-ending and meticulous evaluation of the precepts, their very existence as a caste of recognized jurists, all of this – which to them was the natural order of things – was doomed to extinction.

But for the moment they were too surprised to analyse their emotions. Trained all their lives openly to challenge the law, a process that was as much accepted as it was constrained by rules that limited its scope, they didn't react. Before their very eyes, their young pupil was stepping into their shoes: the most important thing was to listen to what he had to say. It held out the prospect of some wonderful debates after the service, discussions which would last all the way to the marketplace or down to the quay in the little harbour.

Perhaps they were about to interrupt me and point out that I hadn't made any reference to the tradition of the Elders, which was the most glaring omission from what I had said, and to which, carried away by the lava which had finally begun to flow, I had paid little heed. But they didn't have time.

A man came forward into the empty space in the middle of the synagogue, facing the dais on which I was standing. The whole congregation could see him. Dressed in rags, with no coat, no fringes, he was waving his arms wildly – he was one of those simpletons that every village makes allowances for, and are compassionate enough to keep out of harm's way. Although I didn't know his name I had often come across him at street corners, babbling incoherently. But he obviously knew me:

"What have you to do with us, Jesus the Nazarene?"

The Nazarenes are a separate part of the Baptist movement, for whom the Judaean whom I had met by the Jordan said he felt an affinity. But how did this halfwit, who was foaming at the mouth, know that I also felt drawn to the Nazarenes, who loved the Hebrew scriptures above all others, and who had the characteristically Baptist mistrust of any custom that stemmed from the Temple or its Scribes? And then, staring at me with his mad eyes, he went on:

"Have you come to destroy us? I know who you are!"

I know who you are! Apart from God there was only one who knew what I had experienced in the wilderness, the person I had subsequently become, the deep inner transformation that had taken place within me and turned me into a different man – only one, *the Evil One*, the Enemy! He hadn't been idle. He hadn't lost his grip on me, and never would. He was speaking openly through the mouth of this poor wretch, he would be in every person I met, using the weakest of them to assert his authority.

Out there, between the sky and the sand, I had already sensed it: I would have to battle against him every step of the way, face to face, bodies locked together, whether crippled or disfigured by disease. Alone among the astonished congregation, I too knew who I was up against.

"Be silent, and come out of him!"

Crying with a loud voice, the man fell to the floor. When they helped him to his feet he seemed calm and peaceful, more so than ever before.

In a slight state of upheaval, the liturgy followed its course. As they sang the Psalms, everyone was wondering, "What can this mean? Teaching in a way that goes against all the conventions, followed by the healing of a man with an unclean spirit?" Followed... or would it be more accurate to say *corroborated* by this healing? Because in a sense, did the scene they had just witnessed not confirm the innovative nature of my first teaching?

It was a question that even I was unable to answer. At that moment in time, I knew only one thing: that, almost against my will, the insistent inner pressure that had built up inside me while I was in the wilderness had just appeared in public.

From now on, speaking and healing would be associated with every minute of my life. Speaking and healing: outward expressions of the silent, bitter, relentless war that I would have to wage against the Enemy.

A war that would bring me to this quiet night in this tranquil garden in the light of a paschal moon. Now rendered speechless, bleeding from an open wound deep down inside me, the one inflicted on humanity by the Evil One.

13

A Jewish synagogue isn't only a place of prayer, it is where the *knesset*, or community, meets. People exchange ideas, deal with various matters, settle disputes. I managed to slip away without too much trouble, since the congregation's passion for debate meant that their attention soon shifted to other points of interest apart from my recent healing.

Peter, Andrew and Philip wanted to get back to their families in Bethsaida as soon as possible. Feeling no desire to be left alone with my brothers and subjected to their angry remonstrances over my behaviour in the synagogue, I decided to spend the night in this small village that nestled in the north cove of the lake.

Peter was delighted. Once he had sobered up after our visit to Cana, he had heard about the part I had played in ensuring that the wedding passed off smoothly, and discovering that I was familiar with the ways of polite society filled him with a form of infantile pride. Needless to say, the incident in the synagogue had left him dumbfounded, which, given that he had little inclination for deep thought, precluded any chance of him questioning what had really happened.

On the way we were joined by two young men. They had also been at the synagogue in Capernaum, which they preferred to their own – perhaps because of the magnificent mosaics in the entrance hall, which they thought were wonderful. I discovered that they were brothers who often mended their nets with Peter and Andrew, despite the fact that their father, Zebedee, employed men to help fish the lake, something that elevated their status to that of a small local business. My name is John, said the younger one, and this is my brother James.

Their names were so common in Israel that like Simon they were known by a nickname – *Boanerges*, or Sons of Thunder. With youthful insouciance they laughingly told me that they had also spent time with the Zealots, which was when their hot tempers had earned them this Greek-sounding sobriquet – which they found even more flattering. No doubt Zebedee had soon put a stop to these adventurous notions of theirs: having political commitment is one thing, but being two pairs of hands short on a fishing boat is another. As I listened in silence it occurred to me that I, the well-known Pharisee, was walking along the road with three former terrorists – or more likely just three young men embittered by the dead-end existence of the poor, and who would do anything to get away from it.

None of my companions made any reference to the confrontation in the synagogue, which they had all witnessed. Later, I found out that apart from Philip they were all illiterate, something which is more commonplace than people might imagine, despite the fact that every Jewish boy is supposed to be able to make sense of a passage from the Law before he reaches adulthood. They were perfect examples of the silent Israel, in thrall to the coming of the Messiah (fanatical messianism had a firm hold among them) and the restoration of the Kingdom of David – once the Roman occupiers had finally been driven out of God's own country by an armed uprising.

When we got to Bethsaida, Peter told me rather shamefacedly that he was too poor even to own one of the basic, dilapidated huts that are dotted round the shore of the lake. He and his wife lived with her mother: did I mind staying in such wretched surroundings?

Without waiting for me to reply, he led the way into a dark, dismal room. An elderly woman was lying on a bed, struck down by one of those fevers that can bring death in a matter of days. Unable to give voice to his fears, he leant over and wiped the sweat from her face, then stood up and looked at me. In his eyes burned a slightly wild look of expectation, a mute desire.

I straight away knew what he wanted. Unlike the simpleton in the synagogue, this prostrate woman didn't appear to be possessed by Evil. She wasn't screaming and shouting, she posed no threat – she was just going to die.

I took her by the wrist and helped her to sit up. Startled, she got to her feet and just stood there, swaying slightly. Then without a word of thanks she walked out of the room. A moment later we heard her bustling round the fire, wielding kitchen implements and getting the menfolk's supper ready as she had always done.

The room went quiet. The silence lasted for almost the whole meal, as if the Barjona and the Boanerges brothers, who had once contemplated armed insurrection, now felt helpless in the presence of the man who was quietly eating supper with them, dipping his hand in the same dish.

They couldn't begin to make sense of the day's events. Yet they had witnessed them with their own eyes.

When I went and stood on the doorstep, I immediately saw that the womenfolk had done their duty: word had spread from house to house with the speed of female gossip. From every direction came the halt and lame, with the same crazed look of hope in their eyes. Once again the Evil One in them was saying nothing, but I knew that it is he who lies at the root of all disunity – after all, aren't disease and disability simply the result of a body estranged from itself?

Most of them went away healed. Exhausted by my day's work, I collapsed on a pile of straw in a lean-to that had been quickly tidied up for me to use.

I hardly slept. In the middle of the night I got up and quietly left the village, heading in no particular direction.

Once I got to the far side of an olive grove I sat down, as I had in the wilderness. How far away it seemed, that joyous time when I had come so close to being in harmony with God and the cosmos! More than sleep, more than anything else at that moment I needed to find silence again. Then I might be able to give some thought to recent events, try to analyse them. But for now I had to stop thinking. To simply be God's vessel, like water reflects the far-distant stars.

To listen to the silence.

The sun was coming up when I heard Peter's heavy footsteps, felt the breath of his hoarse voice on the back of my neck.

"What are you doing here, Rabbi? Everyone's looking for you!"

Yes. But I am looking for the One who speaks without words.

I struggled to my feet. Without saying a word, I walked back to the lake.

Towards the people who would consume me with their expectations, while others tried to destroy me.

14

There was an important decision to be made, one that I didn't feel quite able to take. Whether to go back to Capernaum, to the workshop, to my brothers' suspicions and my mother's silent reproofs? To the shocked astonishment of my fellow Pharisees, the incomprehension of an ordinary village hemmed in by inherited traditions? I no longer felt able to cope with it. Yet among the confusion, one thing was certain: what I had experienced with John the Baptist and in the furnace of the wilderness had changed me completely. Living under foreign occupation, humiliated, subjugated by a class of priests and theologians who locked the country away in the past – while everything around us was in a state of effervescence – I couldn't huddle up in the comfortable existence of a small-time carpenter from the lakeside any more. Like every Jew I was a son of Elijah. What I had learnt from John the Baptist, from the intuitions that came to me in the wilderness, had awoken the prophet in me. I could conceal it from myself no longer.

Healings? They follow in the footsteps of every prophet. Besides, any number of healers from Egypt or Syria could be found wandering our streets and high roads. I had never had time to study medicine, and magic (which some healers used) fills all Jews with horror. So would I be just one more mountebank in a land already weighed down by sorrows? I knew from the outset that healings could only ever be a partial response to John's call. It wasn't only the sufferings of a few isolated individuals that had to be eased, there was an entire nation waiting to be healed. Only the word could do this – the word of God, with which he created the world and which was alone able to recreate it.

So this was what I decided: for an unspecified period of time I would become one of the wandering preachers who are still very much part of the tradition in Israel. My wealthy friends would support me financially. I decided to travel south in easy stages, taking things as they came. Did my chance companions – Peter and Andrew and Philip, Zebedee's sons – want to come with me? That was up to them. It wasn't me who chose them, but they who had come to me. By not going back to the workshop I would be abandoning my family again, a second rift more drastic than the first – and this time I couldn't use making an initiatory visit to John the Baptist as an excuse.

I was drawn southwards by two men: by the Baptist of course, my first master, the one who lit the vital spark in me. But also the mysterious Judaean, whose thoughtful silences had won me over.

When I told the five Galileans that I was heading for Jerusalem and the mouth of the Jordan, they simply rolled up their coats, slung them over their shoulders and stood at my side. A great feeling of warmth flooded through me: now I was about to leave my closest kin, would these men – with whom I had nothing in common, not social background, education, past life, not even a sense of calling – become a new family for me?

We stopped off at synagogues inland, where there was never any lack of people discussing their business or the Law. With my Pharisee's coat, my long hair, my liking for the Nazarenes, as well as rumours of the healings at Capernaum that had already reached them, I always found the kind of audience I preferred – ordinary working people eager to hear good news of any kind.

Having learnt from experience, this time I just repeated John the Baptist's teachings verbatim: "Convert!" Because of this, people assumed that I was one of his disciples or a Nazarene, which suited me perfectly. I wasn't quite ready to preach the real good news.

Along the way, I helped a few paralysed people to stand on their feet, although they may have simply been exhausted. But it was while we were still in Galilee that I performed a healing whose every detail is still etched in my memory, because it exemplified those that were to come later.

In our country, many people suffer from a skin disease that makes them repulsive to look at, objects of dread, the most unclean of the unclean, whom people refuse to have contact with or even go near. When one of these hideous individuals approached me, my companions moved away in horror, but I let him come. Amazed, he fell at my feet.

"If you choose, you can make me clean…"

He was in such anguish, this man whose illness banished him from his family, his local community and the synagogue for ever! He was one of Israel's living dead, whom no one could touch without being infected by his impurity; the very symbol – and the result – of the fetters that bind an entire people in the name of the Law which it was my responsibility to teach, a fact of which my title of rabbi acted as a constant reminder to everyone I met.

As I bent down to him my stomach churned: the fire that was kindled in the wilderness, the molten lava that had been smouldering ever since… In full view of the horrified passers-by I reached out and touched him, in their eyes becoming as impure as he was. But people had to realize that I wasn't just another healer, that this man's hopes and longings had suddenly come face to face with God's creative power. The poor wretch had appealed against his pitiful condition – I was simply there to help him offer up that cry, to make its powerful voice heard, so he could be living proof that no appeal addressed to God, even the most incoherent, would go unanswered as long as it came from the depths of your soul.

By touching him in public view I proved that he had *already* been purified by the power of his plea, and could no longer infect anyone. It was only fitting that my act should be accompanied by words that would give it its full meaning. Thinking carefully before I spoke, I didn't say: "I make you clean", which would have implied that I was a magician like all the rest. I helped him to his feet.

"I do choose. Be made clean!"

Immediately the disease left him.

And, so that all those standing nearby would realize what had happened, that by using the words "be made clean" I was referring to the source of the healing – because in our language the use of the passive form is a way of describing an act of God without using his name – I went on:

"Go to the Temple. Show yourself to the priests and offer the sacrifice that the Law commands. This will be a testimony to them."

In Israel, even when God himself acts this must still be attested to by the clergy.

A word, a healing. On that day I knew I would always allow the sick to come to me, however deformed they might be, however much they stank. Because healing is the word that best conveys what I had sensed within me when I was alone in the wilderness.

15

The first Passover since my stay by the Jordan was almost upon us, and my companions were eager to get to Jerusalem. Perhaps I was haunted by thoughts of my mother, because I wanted to stop off in Capernaum to see her. This woman was worthy of a son's respect.

I stayed with a client who was also a friend, in his simple little house with its roof made of branches held together by clay. As soon as people discovered I was there it was overrun by a crowd of onlookers, blocking the doorway and overflowing into the street outside. Word of my recent healings had spread though the lanes and alleyways like wildfire. Crushed by the mob, I answered their questions, knowing I had no hope of satisfying the curiosity of these people, who were consumed by a desire for marvels that sprung from feelings of helpless confusion.

Then from outside came the sound of angry protests, followed by shouting. The next moment pieces of wood and rubble began falling into the room – people were smashing the roof, while my host held up his hands to heaven, saying they were destroying his house.

To no avail. A hole appeared through which I could see the sky, and then through it came a stretcher, with a paralytic strapped to it.

No explanation was needed: I understood immediately. Like their paralysed friend, the four men who were lowering him through the roof with ropes felt empowered to break into the house by a sense of urgency that went beyond respect for private property. Yet again, a desire that was strong enough to break through walls, hopes that had once seemed distant yet which were now suddenly in their midst, had materialized for all to see. This man was appealing against a rupture within himself, which had manifested itself in his illness, and he too had already been healed by the power of his plea – all I had to do was bear witness to it. Looking him in the eye, I told him what he needed to hear: that he had already done what he had to do in order to be reunited with God and himself.

"My son" (a term of affection we use to show fellow feeling), "your sins are forgiven."

At the very mention of this word, several Scribes in the room all stiffened.

"Who are you to forgive sins, when this is for God alone to accomplish!"

Blinded by suspicions, they had missed what I actually said – on no account would I have claimed to possess the divine power of forgiveness, which would have been an act of blasphemy. Again weighing my words and using the passive voice, as is usual in our language, I had referred to God without using his name: not "I forgive you", but "*you are forgiven*". By their deafness the Scribes simply revealed the decision that had long been coming to a head in them, that from now on they would regard me as a bitter adversary, not just a colleague who was quite within his rights to interpret the Law.

I didn't reply. It was impossible to have a discussion with these people, the roof of their convictions was firmly sealed against any form of explanation. I turned to the man and told him to stand up, to take his bed and go home.

At my own house, I bowed down before my mother. She didn't say a word – her son wasn't the same since he left the nest.

Without further ado we made our way to Jerusalem. With the Passover approaching, the city was clogged with the usual horde of pilgrims. On the Temple esplanade there was a constant traffic of livestock being taken for ritual slaughter, among all the money-changers who were offering their best rates – because animals bought to sacrifice to the God of Israel had to be paid for in Temple currency, which was the only one accepted there. So these travelling bankers made a vast profit.

These were the very things that John the Baptist had rebelled against from the banks of the Jordan, rejecting costly purification rites and replacing them, in a very visible way, with the water that flows from Mount Hermon (at no cost) – at the same time denouncing the corruption of the mighty Herod and the priests who grovelled to him. Yet what I saw bore witness to just how little impact his words – which would be instrumental in his death – had had. Words were not enough: there had to be deeds, or at least a symbolic gesture (such as a healing), which would show that the axe had now struck the root of the tree.

I looked up. From the ramparts of the Antonia fortress, armed legionaries were keeping a watchful eye on the Temple esplanade, a place where trouble was always brewing. At the first sign of unrest, the slightest hint of any fracas, they would be there, swords drawn. Prevent the buying and selling of livestock? Send the money-changers packing? There would be a riot, blood might be spilt in sight of the Holy of Holies. Yet I wanted to prove to my companions that not only was I one of the Baptist's disciples like them, but that his prediction was coming to pass, the Kingdom was at hand.

So in a quiet corner, out of sight of the police and the legionaries, I overturned one or two tables, took a whip made of cords and swept away a few piles of coins that bore different heads from all across the Empire. The astonished money-changers wasted no time in setting up their stalls again; their only concern was that this lunatic's actions would precipitate the armed intervention that everyone feared. Their vociferous curses were drowned out by the noise of the crowd. Then I slipped discreetly out of the Temple precinct by the side gate and disappeared into the alleyways of the Old Town.

I had done nothing that could be of threat to the main financial and commercial institution in Israel. The important thing was that by acting as I had, I ensured that the booming voice of John the Baptist was heard here as well.

It was on that day, or during those that followed, that I realized that by using this symbolic gesture in the Temple to fulfil what he preached on the Jordan, I had taken John the Baptist's teachings as far as was possible in the Land of Israel. He had provided the inspiration, but I would go further. My first acts of healing were my response to his pessimistic outlook, but I now needed time to establish a new teaching based on these foundations; to open up a new path, one that he might have glimpsed without being able to follow it.

Forgetting nothing, yet travelling beyond it all.

16

Unnoticed among the horde of pilgrims who had come for the Passover, we camped outside the city centre. The money-changers in the Temple might think better of their decision and lodge an official complaint against me – so I decided to keep out of sight. Nonetheless, it was apparent that my fame as a local healer had spread beyond Galilee. A few people recognized me, and asked me to pass on John the Baptist's teachings to them.

As the Passover celebrations were coming to an end, I had just finished one of these discussions when I spotted the elegant figure of the Judaean. He came up to me with a smile: he had been on the Temple esplanade and had seen everything, understood completely, and congratulated me for acting in the name of the Baptist and all Israel by announcing that times were changing. He wanted to introduce me to a friend of his, a prominent Pharisee and a member of the Sanhedrin (the supreme spiritual – and even more so political – authority in the land). Don't worry about his title or his position, he told me. It's true that Nicodemus has a powerful position in Israel, but he's also a fair and upright man who is unimpressed by worldly glory. He would like to talk to the person whom I've told him so much about, so please grant him his wish.

So, just as it was getting dark, in the shadow of the city walls I met this scholarly, intellectually curious and open-minded man. He was blessed with the same unbiased attitude to new ideas as the Pharisees in Galilee, although this was combined with a genuine sense of spiritual enquiry, which couldn't always be said of my fellow northerners. He questioned me at length about the baptism by water practised by John, and I used it as an opportunity to give him an inkling of my experiences in the wilderness. Nicodemus was aware that it wasn't enough to cut down the old tree, but that what the people of Moses urgently needed was a renaissance. Impressed by my healings, he asked if John's baptism was the means of bringing about this rebirth as well as acting as a portent of it, or whether we had to wait for something else.

The fact that this influential man should approach a little rabbi who had already acquired something of a bad reputation in his local area was a sign of real courage. I told him that the next time I came to the capital I would be happy to meet him again, either alone or with our friend the Judaean.

We still haven't left Judaea. What I wanted most of all was to go back and stay with John, who was now baptizing with his disciples at Aenon, near Salem, where the water is abundant. My companions rejected the idea, and it was then that I became aware of the rivalry that existed between them and their former fellow disciples. Although united in their opposition to the Temple, personal ambitions and power struggles were more important to them than the need to join forces! So I let them have their way and allowed them to baptize people who came to listen to me – although I never did this myself, knowing that it was part of a process of renewal that was now obsolete.

But for John's disciples this was going too far, and they complained to him.

"Rabbi," they told him, "the one who was with you across the Jordan, to whom you testified, here he is baptizing, and all are going to him!"

Word reached me that my master was trying to put a stop to this pointless rivalry and pacify his followers. He understood the significance of my refusing to perform baptisms, and that I must have allowed it simply to appease my companions and wasn't gathering disciples around me. He was probably aware that he had gone as far as he could go, that he would now decrease and something else would increase, and that I was ready to open up this new route. He repeated this to anyone who would listen, knowing I would get word of it through the usual grapevine.

There was only one way to bring this petty squabbling to an end, and that was to leave Judaea and go back to Galilee. Protest as they might, I decided to get my companions out of reach of this taste of power, whose bait they had already taken, forgetting who they were, and who John was. We would set off immediately, once again passing through Samaria.

Between Mount Gerizim and Mount Ebal lies a piece of land that Jacob gave to his son Joseph, where there is a spring that feeds a deep well which the local people refer to as "Jacob's Well". Tired out by the journey, I sat by the well while the others went to buy food in Sychar, the nearest town. It was about noon, the sun was beating down from high above and suddenly I felt very thirsty.

A woman appeared, a pitcher on her shoulder. I said to her:

"Give me a drink!"

She could immediately tell from my accent that I was a Galilean, and stepped back.

"How is it that you, a Jew, ask a drink of me, a woman of Samaria?"

With a note of amusement, she then pointed out that I had simultaneously transgressed two laws that were entrenched in our culture: firstly, speaking to a strange woman, unthinkable in a patriarchal society. On top of that I had asked a Samaritan to give me some of her water, although Jews refuse to share anything with these heretics.

She clearly didn't know who I was, since Jewish rumours bypassed this ostracized region in the same way as Jews themselves. But since I insisted, she tried one last gambit:

"But you have no bucket..."

It was true, I was asking to drink from her pitcher, despite the fact that Jews believe that even the utensils used by Samaritans are contaminated by the same impurity that rendered them unclean from the moment their race came into existence. Then she added, provocatively:

"Are you greater than our ancestor Jacob, who gave us the well, and with his sons and his flocks drank from it?"

Left speechless by her words, I didn't reply. Without realizing it, the woman had just expressed something that I would have to include in my new teaching! Ever since meeting the Baptist and spending time in the wilderness, I had had a vague notion that the Law that Moses was given on Mount Sinai had become too great a burden for the Jews to bear. Opening up a new way would take us back to the time of the Jewish patriarchs, *prior to* the Law. We would come down from Sinai and back onto the plain, to hear what God said to Moses *before* he went up the mountain, while he was still prostrated before the Burning Bush.

I owed this sudden revelation to a woman, and a Samaritan woman at that. Before answering I drank deeply from her pitcher. Once I had given it back I told her what I believed, that God didn't dwell on Mount Gerizim or in any other place on earth. She talked about the Messiah: this constant waiting for the coming of the

Messiah and the restoration of the Kingdom of David created confusion in people's minds, provided a pretext for regular and bloody uprisings. I had always been careful not to get involved with these movements, which are so violent, reckless and doomed to failure. Even then I knew that the earthly Kingdom of David would never return. If God were to reign in Israel once more, it would be above all in the hearts of men and women. Yes, there needed to be a restoration, but not a political one – it had to be spiritual, inward.

This had to be at the heart of what I was going to teach.

At that moment my companions reappeared, amazed to find me having a friendly conversation with a strange woman. Alarmed at the sight of them, she ran off.

We were still sitting eating beside the well when a group of men from the nearby town arrived. The woman had spread the word. Would the rabbi from Galilee be kind enough to accept their hospitality... They wanted to invite him to their house, this Jew who wasn't like the others, so they could hear what he had to say, ask him questions.

In spite of my companions' disgusted expressions, I accepted.

So it was that the son of Joseph, brought up in the purest Jewish traditions, spent two days among people who had broken away from Judaism and were hated by his fellow countrymen. Slept under their roof, ate food from the same dish, food that had been prepared by the unclean hands of their womenfolk.

The next day we were back in Galilee.

17

Which of us is able to recall his whole life? All that remains in our memory is a fragment. Interspersed with trips to Jerusalem and a few forays into neighbouring countries, I would spend the next two years in Galilee. Tonight, as my mind ranges back and forth across the years, I am unable to put events in the right order. Yet what does that matter? At this moment, when my life may be drawing to a close, the trifling details that float like spume on the surface of the time I spent wandering are enough to answer the one question that still haunts me: during those months, did my words and deeds succeed in imparting what God expects one of his prophets to impart?

As soon as people knew I was back in the area, word quickly spread and the sick and lame came to me in droves. Most of them went away healed. Like my earliest healings, these were the product of their own hopes, the raging despair that drove them to prostrate themselves before me. I laid my hands on these scrofula sufferers as if power were going forth from me. And there really was power – although I knew that I was neither the source of it nor even its conduit. They came to me after waging a long inner struggle that they were probably unaware had taken place. Not only was I acknowledging their tenacity in this unseen combat, but also the love of a God who never abandons his people.

Whenever I was confronted with blind fatalism, I rebelled. At the time I didn't realize that these healings were my first act of defiance against the established order.

It was only gradually that I came to understand the connection between sickness of the soul and sickness of the body, between the hold that Evil has over sick people and the diseases with which they are afflicted. Through his prophetic acts themselves, every prophet must learn to recognize the reality of the invisible world that confronts him. In turn, I too was unable to avoid this age-old and obligatory apprenticeship.

The memory of one of these healings now comes back to me, although I think it occurred later on.

We were passing through Nain, a large village. We had just gone through the outer gate (Galilee being a land of uprisings, all the villages have fortifications of some kind), when we had to stop for a procession that was making its way out of the village: they were burying someone outside the walls.

On a bier carried by four bearers, the body of a man, still quite young, was just visible. Behind came a woman in mourning clothes. There was no one at her side, she was alone with her grief – a widow who had lost her son, having already lost her husband. The air was filled with the wailing of the large crowd that followed not far behind, the entire population of the village.

Did my thoughts suddenly turn to my own mother, now abandoned by her eldest son, and to whom I must surely have also seemed dead? A shudder ran through me – or was it the lava of the wilderness rising up again? The pain felt by this woman, who was the reflection of all those women in Israel who have someone they have brought into the world cruelly snatched away from them, struck me like a hammer blow. A pain so great at this moment that neither the mother nor the crowd had the strength, even if the thought had occurred to them, to appeal against this death sentence. It was unavoidable, an inevitable step that had to be taken by this young man, whose only need was now the faith in God that his own people didn't possess.

It was left to me to have faith on their behalf. I came forward. Startled, the bearers stood still. I touched the bier.

"Young man, I say to you, rise!"

I was careful not to give death a command, as if I had the power to do so. Through the son I was speaking to his mother and the other mourners. The young man sat up on the bier. As I gave him back to his mother I was aware that I was also restoring, to all those present, the belief that they had momentarily lost, that the One God of Israel is the God of life.

Where does a prophet's power lie? Is he able to imagine for a single moment that he can take the place of the Invisible, who it is his mission to reveal to mankind? Is he able to act like God or even, in his stead, can he create or recreate as He does? To a Jew the very thought is blasphemous, an act of reckless pride, a misunderstanding of the natural order which is quite inconceivable. I would need time to learn to control this power, a power whose source didn't lie in me and as such was all the more precious. Time to offer myself up to it, to offer it openly to other people.

Yet they never truly understood. Like parched ground they were thirsty for marvels, to hail something as a miracle. Among all these Jews, which of them thought to remember that God is God, that I was just a man, an ordinary Jew, and yet no Jew is ordinary when he reaches out his hand to accept power from On High? Very few, judging by my disciples who are sleeping not far away, while I alone keep watch in the night.

Perhaps only the Judaean, who will join us here in the olive grove once he has dismissed his servants and closed the door of the upper room behind him, the room he let us use for the last celebratory supper that I will ever eat with my disciples.

In the minds of the ordinary people, a rabbi is above all a teacher. So it was perfectly natural for me to stop at village synagogues, where there was always a group of idle gossips, squabbling and making pronouncements.

What was I to tell them that wouldn't merely repeat the teachings of John the Baptist? More importantly, how could I offer them a new dish, one that would whet their appetites even when the table was already groaning under the weight of such delicious talk? If I wanted to make them hear and not just listen to me, then the form of what I said would matter as much as the content.

No one sews a piece of unshrunk cloth on an old cloak, for the patch pulls away from the cloak, and a worse tear is made: I was doomed to create something new.

18

From then on a small crowd of people followed me everywhere. Most of them only came a short way, listening and making comments before returning to their homes. Amid all the toing and froing I noticed that the six companions who had been with me since Capernaum had been joined by others. Among them was another Simon, known as "the Cananaean", and Judas, referred to as "Iscariot" – two more names that were given to aspiring Zealots. Yet the fact that there was a faction that advocated violence among my inner circle – the Barjona, the Boanerges brothers, Simon the Zealot and Judas Iscariot – didn't worry me. Like so many others they were just unfortunate individuals struggling to find a new direction in life, a way out of the hopeless situations in which they were trapped, not the least of which was poverty. I never imagined that it wouldn't be long before the terrorists interpreted the fact that these men accompanied me everywhere as tacit support for their movement, so I gladly agreed to take these former rebels with me – my message was aimed at them too.

Suddenly realizing that they were now a group, they began referring to themselves as *disciples*, as they had heard the Baptist's entourage do. It smacked of the animosity that had sprung up on the banks of the Jordan and which had never really gone away, but I took no notice. To hear them talk, the rabbi whose star was on the rise in Galilee now had his own disciples, just like John the Baptist.

Personally I never used the expression, which has Greek connotations. But if I had to have a group of constant companions (as John the Baptist did), if they were to be as much in the public eye as I was, then I wanted this inner circle to have symbolic meaning. Their very presence would become a word, one that ordinary Jewish people could immediately and instinctively understand. They had a role to play in the idea that came to me by the well in Samaria: the woman had likened me to the Patriarch Jacob, whose twelve sons founded the twelve tribes of Israel.

If the farmers who saw us strolling beside their fields and the Pharisees who listened to me in the synagogues were to understand what it was, this dream of mine – to sink the roots of my teaching in the period prior to Sinai, to return to the patriarchs who came before the Law – then I had to have twelve companions. As soon as the right opportunity came along I would make up the number of my faithful followers to a symbolic twelve. This would show that I intended to go back to the vital intuitions that had come to me in the wilderness, the crucible in which Israel was formed.

Yet I never gave up the habit of going off on my own to some deserted place as often as possible, and giving myself up to silence. My companions never understood how important these moments of solitude were to me. As much as I tried to persuade them to come with me, they never did. For me, their eternal inability to understand, which would soon increase twelvefold, has always been the most painful of my failures.

Not long afterwards, the opportunity I was waiting for arose. We were passing one of the customs posts where tax collectors demand extortionate sums from all the small tradesmen and itinerant pedlars who come through. On several previous occasions I had stopped not far from the booth where a Jewish clerk sat, one of the lackeys employed by the great publicans who collaborate with Herod's administration and bleed their fellow countrymen dry – who in return revile them, regard them as unclean in the same way they do lepers. I had noticed then that as I was speaking the man kept looking up and listening to me, a faint glimmer in his eye. Prompted by one of the feelings that I have come to trust unquestioningly since my time in the wilderness, I walked over to him. I don't remember our conversation, but that night he came to see me. He wanted to leave this occupation that filled him with shame, but before he did so, in order to celebrate his resignation as well as to honour the man whom he wished to be his rabbi, he invited me to his house.

Enter the home of a sinner of this kind! Be made unclean by his touch, share food that was tainted by the lure of profit! My disciples' hackles rose, but I insisted. Just like every other sick person, this man had already been purified by the act of approaching me; he had been cleansed of the stain of sin as soon as he left his tax booth and came to me.

He wanted to invite his former fellow tax inspectors to the meal as well, which in a sense would put an official seal on his giving up his occupation. This was something I hadn't been expecting, and my unease seemed to be felt by those around me. Would here be an incident between Zealot sympathizers and collaborators, between devout Jews and sinners sitting round the same table? A complication appeared to be unavoidable, when a delegation of Pharisees from the next village arrived at the door, and (so as not to contaminate themselves) asked some of my companions to come outside.

"Why," they asked authoritatively, "do you eat with tax collectors and sinners?"

Outside, voices were raised. I went out to the little group. Inside me at this very moment, the fire from the wilderness was about to burn down one of the most insurmountable inner boundaries that exist in Israel, the one that insulates a Jew from the world of sinners. In the same way as when I was confronted by the village idiot in Capernaum, the words came by themselves:

"Those who are well have no need of a physician, but those who are sick! I have come to call not the righteous but sinners."

Did they need reminding of what the prophets of Israel had taught – to bring the children back to their father, the lost sheep to the One God? Didn't John the Baptist accept everyone who came to him, both righteous and sinners? He hadn't gone out into the wilderness, any more than I had, simply to preach to men like these who were shut away inside their own notions of justice.

From then on I was happy to eat with people who were ostracized by Judaism. Ever since my time by the Jordan I had been working without a grand stratagem – simply following my instincts, I took each situation as it came. Only later was I able to use these events as the foundation of a teaching that would go beyond and fulfil that of John the Baptist.

My host's name was Levi, although some people called him Matthew. With his arrival the number twelve was reached. So as not to mark them out publicly as my *disciples*, even less as *apostles* (a word not in common use in Judaism), from now on I would just refer to them as *the Twelve* – never imagining that eventually the Twelve would confuse the symbol that they represented with their dream, that of the government of a new Israel in which they would be important ministers.

I think it was at this point that the attitude of some of the Pharisees towards me changed into overt suspicion: a suspicion that would soon become malice, but which would never go as far as threats, at least not in Galilee. I was still one of them, the black sheep of the rabbinic tradition. Even if the most hostile of them regarded me as a poisonous snake that bit the hand that fed it, there were others who were friendly to me until the end. I was always welcome in the synagogues in Galilee, going from one to another.

The axe had fallen on the roots of the tree. It was about to cleave it in two, and everyone would have to take sides.

19

To show people that despite my nonconformity I was still devoted
to the Judaism of our forbears, I decided to go to Jerusalem for a
religious festival. But first I wanted to see my family – our route
took us towards the lake.

There then followed two incidents that would, de facto, cause
me to be excluded from the synagogue.

One Sabbath, so as not to transgress the Law, which forbids all but
the shortest journeys, we were strolling through open fields near a
village. The corn was ripe. As they made their way, my companions
began to pluck heads of grain, rubbing them between the palms
of their hands and eating them. The Pharisees from the village
immediately came and confronted me.

"Look, why are they doing what is not lawful on the Sabbath?"

Observing the Sabbath as a day of rest allows Israel to continue
to exist in the midst of Gentiles. To do even the most minor work,
such as picking corn and rubbing it in your hand, is to infringe the
Law. So was the young rabbi intending to overturn one of the pillars
of Jewish identity? No rabbi can interpret the Law in such a way
that it is demolished. What subtle argument would I use to justify
my companions' act of sacrilege? I turned to my fellow rabbis:

"Have you never read what David did when he and his companions were hungry and in need of food? It was when Abiathar was high priest."

They nodded. I was quoting the classic texts, answering their question with another, so the debate was proceeding according to the rules. I went on:

"He entered the house of God and ate the bread of the Presence, which it is not lawful for any but the priests to eat, and he gave some to his companions."

I knew what they were going to say: firstly you are misinterpreting the text. Secondly, can any Jew liken himself to King David, or his companions to his own? Suddenly I was utterly weary of these discussions of theirs, which always followed the same predictable course and came to the same unvarying conclusions. It was never my intention to challenge the Law, simply to argue that in an emergency, human needs take priority. I was now able to see far beyond their narrow logic, I wanted to make humanity human again. To curtail any more exchanges, I added abruptly:

"The Sabbath was made for humankind, and not humankind for the Sabbath."

They just stood there in amazement. So was what people said about him true? In Capernaum he had forgiven a paralytic his sins, and now here he was, no longer content just to query the Law, as was right and proper – no, he was claiming that mankind didn't have to submit to God by obeying it, but that people could submit *it* to their every passing need!

Without replying, they turned on their heels and went back to the village.

When I arrived there shortly afterwards, the villagers (who knew nothing of what had happened) invited me to their synagogue. They wanted to hear what I had to say, ask me questions, have a debate: to do what every Jew does on the Sabbath – open the sluice gates of the living Law.

No sooner had they sat down than the Pharisees asked a man with a withered hand that was hanging limply by his side to join them. Then, smiling, they watched me: what was I going to do? A self-satisfied healer blinded by his own importance, thirsting for fame, would I fall into their trap?

This had to stop. I told the man to stand in the open in front of the dais where everyone could see him.

Unlike the people I had encountered before, this man hadn't come to me, he wasn't asking for anything, and hadn't taken the outward, visible step that was a sign of inner healing. Before he could even think of regaining the use of his hand, I had to make him want to be himself again.

All Jews are familiar with the interminable debates about the observance of the Sabbath. When a farmer's only donkey, without which he can't cultivate his land, falls into a ditch, is he allowed to pull it out using a hoist? The Essenes say no – using ropes or a ladder would contravene the Law. But if a human being falls down a well, do you let him or her drown in the muddy water without trying to help? Anyone would say no, naturally. The Essenes allow you to throw them a coat, so you avoid having to carry a ladder to the well. The strictest Pharisees side with this view, while others allow anything to be used, ladders or ropes, if it means a human life can be saved.

So, confronted with a man with a withered hand, which school of thought would he follow, this young rabbi who was becoming something of a liability? After all, no one's life was in danger in this synagogue today, was it?

The Pharisees waited.

I spoke to them sharply:

"Is it lawful to do good or to do harm on the Sabbath, to save life or to kill?"

Was the Law opposed to fighting the Evil One, who dances attendance on us throughout our whole lifetime? The Pharisees didn't reply, refusing to continue a discussion based on these terms. Yet again I was attempting to circumvent the rules, to shift the interpretation of the Law onto unfamiliar territory. For them it wasn't a question of Good versus Evil, a fine problem as old as the world itself and which even Job wasn't able to solve. It was a matter of knowing precisely where interpretation of the Law ends and the realm of God begins. They wanted to establish reference points as if they were surveying a piece of land, whereas in the wilderness I had met Evil face to face, a decisive experience that bore no resemblance to solving mathematical equations. Faced with Evil I hadn't tried to reason, I had wept. These jurists and I didn't speak the same language – they were trying to lock me away inside their reasoned arguments, and this poor wretch in his paralysis, like a surveyor marking out boundaries with a chain.

Anger surged up in me like a tidal wave. I caught the man's eye: he seemed to realize that his withered hand was just an excuse for a debate, and that the real issue was something quite different, something that was buried deep down inside him and all the other members of the congregation. Was he going to be the one to choose between the advocates of ropes and ladders and the partisans of the coat? Of course not. Did he see a connection between the power of the Enemy and his withered hand?

Quietly I said to him:

"Stretch out your hand."

In full public view, he stretched it out and it was restored.

I had the answer to my question, and the Pharisees had the answer to theirs.

By once more giving a sick human being priority over the tenets of the Law, I had sided *with* the ordinary people and their sufferings against the hard line taken by the Essenes and some of the Pharisees. Cloaked in their dignity, they got up and went outside where they started conspiring bitterly among themselves.

There is no legal body that has the power to bar a Jew from the synagogue, thus excluding him from society as a whole. The Pharisees are not answerable to any central authority: each of them follows the dictates of his conscience, although always within the bounds of the tradition. So was I claiming to be a master in my own right, rejecting the culture of compromise that is the lifeblood of Judaism? Word spread quickly round the hills of Galilee: although nothing was said officially, it was made clear to me that I was no longer welcome at gatherings on the Sabbath, or at any others that were held within the walls of the *Beth ha-sefer*. People would still call me Rabbi, but from now on my synagogue would be the sky over Galilee, my teaching would be done in the houses of a few friends.

But I had other things on my mind: we had almost reached the lake and my family home.

Driven back by a succession of healings, the Evil One was working on his plan of campaign for future battles.

20

In Capernaum I stayed at the house of a sympathetic minor official. It wasn't as convenient as the synagogue with its dais and benches – we were crushed into one room, and the crowd overflowed out of the door. I saw a few familiar faces, one or two Pharisees from the local area who were there to listen to their pupil, who dared challenge the rules of the Sabbath. But I saw no sign of my brothers or my mother.

There was such a crush that we couldn't even eat. It was then that someone came and told me that my family had arrived en masse to take me away.

"Your mother and your brothers and sisters are outside, asking for you."

I looked at the people sitting round me, their worried faces, the helpless expressions that bore witness to their despair. I had a duty to them, they were the family of my rebirth. Speaking loudly enough to be heard outside, I said:

"Who are my mother and my brothers?"

And I made a sweeping gesture round the crowd.

"Here are my mother and my brothers!"

Later, people would claim that I added, in a quiet voice: "Whoever hears the word of God and abides by it, whoever does the will of God is my brother and sister and mother."

How could I have said such a thing? Rebuke my own family, who were devout Jews? Rebuke my mother, who had given me everything? Didn't they realize that I wasn't disowning my mother or my brothers, but that from this moment on I would be begotten with each new day by all these desperate people whose hopes and expectations broke down my inner barriers one after another? Those who attribute these words to me, words which no son, no Jew would ever think of saying, are probably the same ones who even then had taken the name of disciples, who wanted to keep me for themselves and use me as a pretext for living apart from everyone else.

My mother and brothers went away, the bonds of flesh between us sundered. A family that was wounded, yet which had the support of the villagers who couldn't understand why the local carpenter, Mary's son, now refused to speak to her or to his brothers, James, Joses, Judas and Simon – and preferred to create imaginary relatives from among the people who came to listen to him wherever he went.

That night, I was told how my mother and brothers had reacted.

"He has gone out of his mind." When their neighbours asked, this was how they explained the behaviour of someone whom they had seen grow up into a respected local figure.

Out of my mind... In other words, mad. They were trying to put me into a category by using the only feasible explanation: mental illness. I wasn't a bad son, just mentally disturbed.

But the next day I was confronted with another attempt to explain my behaviour, one for which I was quite unprepared.

Drawn by rumours of my healings, which were now arousing the interest of the authorities, some Scribes came down from Jerusalem. These weren't minor intellectuals like those who live locally, but experienced theologians. They set up a form of temporary court of inquiry outside the synagogue and passed swift judgement:

"He has a demon!"

So they didn't regard me as mad, but possessed by the Devil. This was a very serious accusation. I don't know if they had ever been involved in hand-to-hand combat with the Evil One as I had, but they were apparently in a position to enact laws against him. In their directory of crimes this made me an outcast, even worse than a leper. Once they had passed sentence the demon would have to be cast out then and there, and if that didn't succeed I would be sent into the wilderness to die. I decided to stand up to this tribunal of theirs.

They greeted me as a Pharisee come to present his case, and levelled the accusation:

"It is by Beelzebul, the ruler of the demons, that you cast out demons!"

I saw that they were – quite rightly – treating my healings as part of the war against Satan, and replied with a question, as is customary:

"If a kingdom is divided against itself, how can that kingdom stand? If a town or a tribe is divided, will it not fall?"

It was a telling blow. These shrewd lawyers immediately realized that they were in a weak position. But I still had to convince the local people, so I drove my point home:

"How can Satan cast out Satan? If he has risen up against himself, how can his kingdom stand?"

This time, all those present understood: these high and mighty scholars from the capital had underestimated the little country rabbi! They were looking down their noses at the mud-spattered Pharisees from Galilee as usual. Did they really think this crude trick would fool Joseph's son, who was educated here in the village by our own learned men, who were just as good as they were

– and here was proof! And I sensed I was in a position to give the death blow:

"If I cast out demons by Beelzebul… by whom do your own exorcists (who are so quick to do their work) cast them out? Therefore will they not be your judges?"

I had gone from accused to accuser. If they didn't immediately answer my question with another, it meant that they admitted defeat. For a moment there was silence, and then they stood up, as rigid as their law, and made their way out of the village – past the ironic smiles of the villagers who watched them leave.

I had been granted a reprieve. The local Pharisees who had taken my side were seen to be vindicated, while the others champed at the bit. The ordinary people of Galilee, meanwhile, were overjoyed to see me stand up to the authorities from Jerusalem, and I knew I had won them over – even if it was unthinkable to show this in public.

The next day I set off for Jerusalem. A group of people from the village came part of the way with me. When they turned to go back, I said solemnly:

"Prophets are not without honour, except in their home town, and among their own kin, and in their own house."

Home town, kin, house: in this land of honour and dishonour I was openly admitting that I had lost the three things that lie at the heart of every Jew.

Along the way we heard the terrible news – John the Baptist had been arrested by Herod's police and imprisoned in the fortress of Machaerus. Knowing how easily influenced the King was, and how much his wife hated the Baptist, we all knew what it meant: within a few weeks, perhaps a few days, the voice of this great prophet would be silenced for ever.

21

Tonight, although I am aware of the distance I have travelled from the banks of the Jordan to the quiet of this garden and its kindly olive trees, I no longer remember the order in which my stays in Galilee actually happened. When I got to Jerusalem I would be seeing the Judaean again, and I admit that the prospect dispelled my sadness at the loss of my master, as well as finding myself an outcast in the place where I grew up.

The city was the same as ever, its throng of pilgrims, idlers and priests rubbing shoulders with the Roman soldiers who quietly strolled the streets. Since the rebellion led by Judas of Galilee twenty years earlier, the region had enjoyed a period of peace that no one wanted to see come to an end. I met my friend just outside the western part of town where he lived, and explained that I wanted to stay for a few days: where could I find accommodation for my disciples and myself? He suggested I go with him to Bethany, a village less than three kilometres away. He knew a wealthy landowner there whose property, which was close to Jerusalem without being too close, would provide the peace and quiet I was looking for.

Lazarus gave me a warm welcome, perhaps more than customary Jewish hospitality required. The Judaean had already told him about me, as he had Nicodemus. He said I could stay as long as I liked, that from now on I should treat his home as my own. His sister Martha, who never seemed to rest, acted as mistress of the household and looked after the domestic affairs. Lazarus had a great many clients and colleagues in Jerusalem, and she made it a point of honour to entertain them royally. Mary, his other sister, wasn't as assertive as Martha, and seemed to be constantly at her beck and call. This traditional family were soon quite attached to me, and it became my second home, taking the place of the one I had lost.

In Jerusalem no one found it unusual that a disciple of John the Baptist, particularly one who was a Nazarene, didn't offer sacrifices at the Temple, although it was the done thing at least to put in an appearance during major religious festivals, which for me was an opportunity to remind myself of my ordinary Jewish roots, something I enjoyed. The Judaean showed me round his native city, which he knew like the back of his hand. As it was the Sabbath, would I like to go to the bathhouse with him, a Roman habit that sat well with the old Jewish tradition of ritual cleansing? He took me to the pool of Beth-zatha, an enormous public baths in a lush green spot just outside the walls, by the Sheep Gate.

Around the pool itself were five porticos, beneath which lay many invalids – blind, lame and paralysed. With a smile, the Judaean told me that these poor souls were waiting for the water – which came from a deep source – to start bubbling: it was commonly believed that at this moment an angel of God went down to the pool. Who-ever stepped in first after the stirring of the water was made whole, freed from whatever disease they had. It was evidence not only of the power that superstition had over these desperate people, but also of that of the healers who took advantage of this obscurant-ism, to which their fellow elite, the priests, turned a blind eye.

Lying on a mat in the midst of all the suffering humanity on display in the shade of the porticos was a paralysed man who kept staring at me. I asked someone nearby about him, and they said the man had been coming there every day for the last thirty-eight years. I caught his eye: in it was written the tragedy of a life spent waiting, which filled me with compassion. I asked him:

"Do you want to be made well?"

As always I made sure to use the passive form, which leaves the salvation of the body or soul firmly in God's hands. Probably noticing that I wasn't claiming to heal him with a charm or magic spell like the others, he replied resignedly:

"Sir, I have no one to put me into the pool when the water is stirred up, and while I am making my way, someone else steps down ahead of me."

So for thirty-eight years this man's life had been made up of wishing and hoping! Without ever losing faith in God, he had waited for his appeal to be heard. And I had the vast yet tenuous power to tell him that today his wait was over, that his years of perseverance had healed him inwardly – the fact that his paralysis had gone attested to the depth of his faith. So as not to be overheard, I leant forward and said:

"Stand up, take your mat and walk."

Without replying he stood up, put his mat under his arm and headed towards the main door.

Beside me, the Judaean had witnessed everything. Taking me by the arm, he dragged me behind a nearby pillar. After recent events in Galilee, it would be best if this healing were attributed to the angel of God rather than to me. On his way out, the former paralytic was quickly surrounded by the crowd. An argument was already underway, and a loud, imperious voice drifted across to where we were standing:

"It is the Sabbath; it is not lawful for you to carry your mat!"

It was some dignitary or other, using a visit to the baths to remind everyone of their legal obligations on this hallowed of days. Listening hard, I just caught the last few words of what was being said. The paralytic was standing up for himself:

"The man who made me well said to me, 'Take up your mat and walk!'"

"Who is the man who said to you, 'Take it up and walk'?"

The paralytic looked round. He didn't know who it was, for his healer had disappeared into the crowd.

The next day I saw him in the Temple, where he had made a sacrifice to bear witness to his healing. As I walked over he recognized me.

"See, you have been made well," I whispered in his ear. "Do not sin any more, so that nothing worse happens to you."

Once again I had weighed my words. If he had been made well it was because he was ready. Yet he had to remain on guard: against Evil no victory is ever final. But, probably still under the influence of Jewish superstitions, he didn't seem to hear me, because the next moment he went over to a group of worthies and pointed me out.

The Judaean urged me to leave the Temple precincts, in fact the city immediately, even to avoid Galilee until people (in Jerusalem as well as by the lake) had forgotten about all the times I had contravened the laws of the Sabbath.

Once we had crossed the Jordan, we headed along the east bank towards the area of the Decapolis, taking care not to come into contact with the local population, who were mostly Gentiles. This was the first time I had had to hide, to flee the authorities. It wouldn't be the last.

But tonight, in the light of the paschal moon, I am fleeing no longer.

22

I think we had just arrived in Galilee when some of the Baptist's disciples caught up with us. They brought a message from their master, who had sent them to ask me:

"Are you the one who is to come, or are we to wait for another?" In the depths of his dungeon, this is what he wanted to know.

John's question was a sign of inner lassitude. What could I say to the man who had witnessed my conversion in the wilderness, and was now trying to catch a last glimmer of hope in the dark night of his soul, as well as that of Israel, before he died? As it happened, there were some sick people among the small crowd who had gathered to listen to me. Witnessed by John's messengers, who could hear what I was saying, I sent them away whole.

"Go and tell John what you have seen and heard: the blind receive their sight, the lame walk, and the poor have good news brought to them!"

As usual I was careful not to tell the prisoner in Machaerus that it was *me* who gave the blind their sight, *me* who caused the lame to walk, but that I had simply been present when these healings took place. Even my teaching, which was now departing more and more from his own, was not truly mine: the good news *was brought* to the poor, it was between them and God.

John would understand.

But it was too late. Not long afterwards, news of the death of the bare-chested prophet spread across the whole country – with gruesome details of the furtive and shameful way in which his head had been severed from his body in a dark cellar then presented on a platter to Herod, who was feasting with his court.

The Evil One had won this battle.

It affected me even more deeply than my disciples. With John dead, Elijah's mantle had to be picked up from the pool of blood where it lay. I owed it to my master, to myself and to every Jew. Assuming this mantle would mean teaching, first and foremost throughout the length and breadth of Galilee, where I would have to travel constantly in order to make my voice heard.

And why not Judaea? Even Jerusalem? Perhaps, but that would come later. What of healings? For me, these weren't performed with a view to establishing my reputation, but to bring about something entirely new, not simply to restore a few individuals to health. I was well aware that what attracted people's attention were so-called miracles – how could it be otherwise? Yet I knew that my word alone could give meaning to these different healings.

Teaching... With John dead, I was no longer bound inwardly by the vow of loyalty and respect that a disciple owes his master. I could find my own style, give voice to what had been simmering away inside me since my time in the wilderness. What of the Pharisees and their dialectics? I had shown what little regard I had for the fetters of their tradition. In the end it would come down to a confrontation between them and myself, that was inevitable – but I would deal with that when the time came! "Never cut yourself off from the people," was what Hillel said. I had to create a language that was both ancient and modern, one that could be understood by everyone, whatever their level of education and culture, ordinary people as well as the intelligentsia. A universal language, with enough depth so people could use it to shine light on their dreams, discover different viewpoints that matched their individual needs, and which would bring them to the gates of the Ineffable – beyond which everyone must travel alone.

From now on the *form* of my teaching would be something I had to consider in incisive detail.

New wine must be put in new wineskins.

Part II

Born to Be Reborn

Pray that all this good of ours might turn to evil,
And all the evil to good...

Saint-John Perse

23

From the saddles of their camels, the nomadic Arabs, whose way of life takes them all over the Mediterranean region, have always looked down somewhat pityingly on my fellow countrymen, whose backs are constantly bent over their hoes. Natural traders, their hands are always on their swords, ready to raid and plunder under the remorseless desert sun. These warriors and profiteers have nothing but contempt for the Jews, who are chained to the ploughshare. Besides, the colourful peasant dialect that these clodhoppers speak doesn't lend itself to commerce, does it?

So how could I communicate with these hard-working sons of the soil? First I had to tell them they were like the salt that they dug up in blocks from the ravines, where they knew it was to be found. A mere pinch was enough to flavour the food on their table, while a handful would preserve the fish they caught in the lake almost indefinitely. I had to teach them to love themselves again, remind them that since the time of Abraham, Jacob and Moses they had been the custodians of a divine promise that is only as enduring as their faith.

Then I would liken them to the only oil lamp in their dilapidated hovels, which they didn't light just to hide it under the bushel basket that they use to measure grain. Despite their being disheartened

111

at having their hopes constantly dashed, weighed down by their narrow existence, I would tell them that they could still be a light to shine forth before people everywhere, simply by the radiance of their everyday acts.

I would give them back their self-confidence, remind them that no Jew is ordinary, because he bears within him, engraved in his very being, the mark of God's creative act and his call to be reunited with him. I began to realize that my healings were more than just acts of compassion – better than any speech, they demonstrated how I meant to leave John the Baptist's pessimistic vision behind. Unlike him I hadn't come to proclaim a desolating fire, the end of the world in a fiery furnace, but a new creation like the one at the beginning of time: a rebirth.

To be born again: as Nicodemus had sensed, this was exactly what my teaching had to offer to a people whose heart and soul were diseased. To stay the same, while becoming a new person. Never denying what had gone before, yet going beyond it. Now I was a wandering prophet: I wouldn't only speak in order to impart, to tell things as they were and how they came to be. What I said had to *bring into being* something that didn't exist, or at least not yet. For a Jew, to speak is to create – pronouncing the name of something that is only a hope or an expectation, transforms it into a reality.

Despite their unshakeable sense of exclusivity, the Jews have been influenced by initiatory religions whose origins lie in the East. Unlike the uninitiated, the neophyte is no longer blinded by the bright light of the mystery; he enters into its depths, and the scales of doubt fall from his eyes.

Yet by opening up the gates of knowledge, initiation destroys the mystery itself.

I had to lead the people who listened to me to the threshold of the mystery that had been revealed to me in the wilderness, while preserving it in its inviolate state. The One God has no name, words cannot describe or tell of Him. By forever pontificating about God, the Scribes shroud the mystery in a web of dialectic, each strand of which blocks off the path that leads to its meaning rather than opening it up.

Instead, my words would be like a mirror, which would take my audience back to the source of the light without dazzling them. By its very simplicity and clarity, this original meaning would reveal many others, all as varied and unfathomable as human nature itself.

Yet by simply making assertions, I risked overestimating the unique calling of the men and women who sat listening to me. What I had to do was not proclaim, but *evoke*, not reveal but *propose*.

Our rabbis prefer to teach by way of short, succinct maxims. This is suited to a culture where nothing is written down; they can be passed on down the ages, never at risk from fire or damp – unlike parchment or papyrus, those luxuries reserved for the wealthy, and as insubstantial as their wealth.

These maxims represent the library of the poor, who preserve them on the bookshelves of their memories. Yet even if a maxim is inscribed in the mind, a parable surpasses it by appealing to the imagination, casts a spell over all who hear it.

I can't remember when this certainty first dawned on me, but it transformed the way I taught.

Without disregarding maxims, from now on I would teach in parables.

More than any Jew had done before.

We were walking along one of the stony paths that run beside the crops in our part of the world. A farmer was scattering seed far and wide across the ploughed earth of his field. The birds were eyeing his every move, and he kept shouting to scare them away, so they didn't take their share of the seed as soon as it landed. The sun was high in the sky, blazing fiercely in the still air.

From this familiar, everyday sight came the first of my parables. Asking the small crowd who were with me to sit down beside the track, I pointed to the man, striding out across his field.

"Listen! A sower went out to sow..."

I showed them the seed that had fallen by the wayside, which the birds swooped down and ate. Then the seed that fell among the stones that were dotted across the field – it would spring up quickly but wouldn't take root. And the seed that fell among the thorns that the farmer hadn't bothered to pull up – and which would grow tall and choke it. I pointed to the next field, which had been sown not long before, where the young shoots had no depth of soil and were scorching in the sun. Finally I painted a picture of the ripe, fat, healthy ears of corn that would eventually grow out of the good soil, but which were still just a distant hope.

Amazed to hear something as commonplace as sowing seeds treated in such a theatrical way, they turned to me, expecting to be told the real meaning. So I exclaimed:

"Let anyone with ears to hear listen!"

Yet did they actually have ears? Judging by their reactions, the blank expressions, the disgruntled looks, I could see they didn't – they had listened but not heard. They expected much more from the gifted young rabbi whose fame was spreading by the day than a description of a field, a detailed commentary on a ploughman at work!

Some of them shrugged, then got up and walked away.

From the questions asked by those who remained, it was clear that all they had grasped from the parable was the moral behind it. Some of them compared themselves with the stony ground, others with that by the wayside, with the good soil or the poor; what they saw in these images was a reflection of themselves, whether flattering or unflattering. Having stopped at the signpost they hadn't even noticed which direction it was pointing in – that very few seeds ever fall into good soil and bear fruit. That many were the stumbling blocks, the risks and dangers. That in a sense the seed had to work with the soil in its struggle to survive.

That being born again required an effort, that it would take time; that they shouldn't expect help from me or anyone else, that everything had to come from them.

Some of the local Pharisees were there. From their worried expressions I could tell that these experts were busy pondering another matter, one they considered fundamental. Some rabbis also tell little stories which stick in people's minds, but it is always a way of illustrating or interpreting the Law. However, because the parable I told about the sower stood on its own, the authority of its teaching derived from the fact that it was self-evident. Everywhere I went in Galilee, this subtle argument was just one of many with which they would take issue. It was part of a case file that was being built up, and which was already lying on the desk of the Pharisees in Jerusalem, waiting to be dealt with.

We set off again in awkward silence. As soon as we stopped to rest, the people who were still there came over to me, led by my disciples. So what was this imagery supposed to mean?

As if mutilating a flower by plucking off its petals one by one, I had to explain the parable to them in minute detail. With a heavy heart, dragging my feet over every word, I reduced the mystery of their lives to its moral aspect, the only one that seemed to have penetrated their skulls. The Twelve were the most dull-witted of all: perhaps they were already beginning to suspect that by offering them a choice that only affected them individually, I had no intention of ever seizing power in Israel.

I burst out:

"Do you not understand this parable? Then how will you understand all the parables?"

At this moment I was confronted by my isolation in all its enormity. I thought I had left everything behind – village, family, home; all that remained was a single vision, that of sharing the fire that had been kindled in me in the wilderness. I couldn't hold it back any longer, so who was I to pass it on to?

The Twelve, these self-appointed disciples who were proud to be among the entourage of a rabbi whom they apparently believed could fulfil their every expectation, had proved themselves incapable of following the path that had been opened up by my first parable. It was then I realized that their failure to understand would go on sapping my inner strength until the end.

Until tonight, when they lie sleeping a stone's throw away, leaving me alone in the dark night of the soul that is now my lot.

24

And yet I didn't seem isolated, quite the reverse. Rabbis in Israel
have always led a sedentary life; those such as Hillel, who never
left Jerusalem in all his forty years of teaching. The pupils they
choose come to them, gather at their feet. But no one had ever seen
a wandering rabbi, one who went from farm to village, wearing
out his feet on the winding roads and paths of Galilee. The poor
farmers were overjoyed – perhaps even flattered – when a young
doctor of the Law took the time to stop and have a conversation
with them beside their fields, or in the yards of their humble dwell-
ings. Thanks to them a good reputation went before us, and we
were made welcome everywhere. We were fed, sometimes allowed
to sleep in a barn.

Yet wherever you go in this country of ours, the wilderness is
never far away, even in the area around the lake. Among the vast
expanses of dry grass roamed by a few scattered herds of goats,
the bare hillsides that soon give way to rocky plains stretching
into the distance, we couldn't always find somewhere to stay. And
when we broke our journey in a small town, there was always the
problem of logistics – because as well as the Twelve, our numbers
were often temporarily swelled by a contingent of total strangers
who also had to be fed and housed. It surprised me when wealthy

landowners, dignitaries and occasionally even tax collectors invited us to eat with them and stay in their homes. Their wives were most solicitous, and dispatched servants with baskets of bread, figs and dried fish after us as we travelled on. Some of them sometimes came with us as far as the next overnight stop.

I never turned them away. Among the simple folk, and even my disciples, my openness to them sometimes created a slight awkwardness. I took no notice, refusing to treat these women as if they were of no significance. In return they showed extraordinary nobility of spirit, and by being with us in public they sometimes broke very strong taboos.

I think it was this maternal presence that caused me to gradually renounce my Nazirite vows. Whenever they smilingly offered me wine from one of the wineskins that had been brought from their storeroom for me, I let them fill my cup and savoured the precious liquid. Thus I relinquished what had been passed down to me by my parents, as well as my final link with the sternness of John the Baptist.

As time went by, a whole crowd of people began to revolve around me as if in concentric circles. The inner circle represented by the Twelve – who knew that without the circle of my friends and benefactors I would never have been able to carry out my mission – took shameless advantage of this life of ease and material security that far exceeded anything that the drudgery of their everyday existences could have offered. The third and outer circle of occasional listeners helped widen my audience beyond the reach of my voice; this group of hostile or sympathetic critics soon formed my most reliable source of protection against the hatred of the authorities.

People also made generous donations of money, so we needed someone to look after our savings. From the Twelve I chose Judas to keep the common purse and hand out the customary alms on our behalf. He was a good choice, for his honesty has always been above reproach.

Although constantly surrounded by supporters, opportunists and listeners, I still felt as isolated as I had been in the wilderness – except perhaps during a brief springtime in Galilee, whose memory remains with me as a moment of great hope that was followed by bitter disappointment.

Outstanding teachers that they are, the Pharisees have always tried to summarize their teaching in a single word, like a rudder that leaves a trail in the wake of the mighty ship of the commandments. So had my first parable failed? I tried to think of a unique and powerful expression that would best sum up the fire that had been burning in me since I was in the wilderness. After the encounter with the Evil One from which I emerged the victor, I had been filled with a secret sense of joy. It was this that should form the basis of my reform of the Law. I couldn't just be the herald of a long list of laws and obligations that would be an unbearable and painful burden, I had to admit people into the mystery, the great festival of reconciliation with God and themselves, offer them rules that were not oppressive but light as air, the joy of living, the key to a flourishing life that was within everyone's reach, particularly those marginalized by society.

When I was in the wilderness I had had an intuition, which told me that there was a specific way of approaching things, people and situations. I now felt able to express this in a single word: joy, a joy that was attainable.

This word had to encapsulate all the others by which my teaching would finally set me apart from John the Baptist, whose doom-mongering only caused fear and trembling.

So I could at last be myself, openly and for all to see.

There were many people there that day, spread like a cloak around a small knoll perched above the lake. I sat on a blue-grey rock and looked round at the Twelve, gathered at their master's feet, and at the other faces on the slope, some of which I knew, some that were unknown to me. It was as if all Galilee had come together on this little hilltop. And there in the silence, emboldened by all the expectant faces, I began:

"Joyful…"

25

Joyful, or *toubayon* in our melodious Aramaic tongue, refers to simple, everyday happiness. Joyful... I had to turn this word, which was so familiar from the Psalms and the words of the wise men of Israel, but which had become unfamiliar to Jews living under tyranny, into a chant, a threnody. This is how I would begin:

"Joyful are the poor, for theirs is the Kingdom of Heaven!"

I felt all eyes converge on me. In Israel, wealth is at once the symbol and proof of divine blessing, whereas poverty shows that this has been withdrawn. So the poor – my audience – were now the beneficiaries of God's goodwill! This was exactly what I wanted to set in motion – a reversal of the existing order. As was customary, I hadn't used the holy and unpronounceable name, but one of the many circumlocutions with which a Jew speaks of God without referring to him: *Power* or *Kingdom of Heaven*, the On-High, the *shamayim* that were the focus of the hopes and desires of an entire nation. I went on:

"Joyful are those who hunger and thirst, for they will be filled, joyful are those who mourn, for they will be comforted and will laugh!"

I could feel the small crowd beginning to rise up like dough. In this land that was a stranger to famine, what they most hungered for was God's Justice, a loss they constantly mourned. Ever since Rachel had wept for her sons, a mother inconsolable because they were gone for ever, every Jew had been weeping, yet here I was, opening the gates of laughter for them!

I noticed that the Zealots among my disciples had gathered round to listen. They were outraged that a land registry had been set up in Israel, where an inventory of land cannot be taken because it belongs to God alone. So it was for the benefit of these former advocates of violence that I added:

"Joyful are the meek, for they will inherit the earth!"

This land had been given to Abraham long ago, a gift that was later reaffirmed to Moses, yet neither of these Patriarchs ever benefited from it; the second of them died at the moment he caught sight of it in the distance. When would they realize that the Promised Land wasn't the one they wanted to purge of its Roman occupiers, that it didn't exist anywhere except within them – that they themselves were God's land?

Joyful, joyful... lulled by the music of the word, I spoke to them of mercy granted and mercy received, of love that is shared, reconciliation as the wellspring of life. Of the purity of a heart scorched by the flame (as mine had been in the wilderness), and which is thus able to discern something of the One who remains invisible to the naked eye. I serenaded them with images of the world to come, where the dreams of the prophets would finally come true.

By allowing it to burst forth in front of all these people, I suddenly appreciated the sheer magnitude of the joy I had discovered in the wilderness, through utter destitution and a violent and agonizing encounter with the Evil One. I realized that the tears I had shed there helped me to empathize with the pain and suffering that I found along the way, but also that they had cleansed me inwardly. A happiness that was not of this world – one that had always been absent from my life and for which I had longed for many years – a happiness beyond compare now manifested itself to me. I sensed that it was strong and yet fragile, that the Enemy would do everything within his power to destroy it, that it might not endure. It was of this that I had to speak, in these early days when everything seemed simple, I had to open up the way for them, clear the obstacles from their path.

Like John the Baptist I was foretelling the end of a world, but also the birth of a new one.

The local Pharisees in the crowd said nothing. The prophets have always spoken of the *ebionim*, the legendary "remnant" of the poor of Israel. Meekness, mercy and justice lay at the heart of the prophets' teaching, but I was going much further. For one thing, my law of happiness had nothing in common with the Jewish Law, because it didn't seek to establish rules for human behaviour. Happiness is not a law, at most it is an aim, an aspiration shared by the whole human race. It was all too easy to replace the strictness of the commandments with a hazy, utopian ideal of happiness – so to them I was just another fashionable preacher.

Yet the most important question was this: who were my words intended for? The poor, the hungry, the afflicted… Did I want to start a popular uprising of these people, whom the ruling class kept in a tenuous state of peace by the use of force? Or was this happiness I promised just a way of tempering the Zealots' perpetual dissatisfaction, so they would renounce violence and take a "meek" approach, which would just be another form of subservience? For the first time abandoning the sacredness of the land of Israel to the greedy collaborators who prostrated themselves before the ungodly occupier?

So where did I stand on the complex political chessboard of this little country ruled by Rome?

Scattered among and standing out from all the approving smiles, were puzzled eyes that looked daggers at me, pursed lips, stony expressions – all weighing my every word, assessing its political or social implications. But I was elsewhere… Joyful, joyful!… Like a flag floating in the breeze, my words were enfolded with joy. Swept away by the tide of lava that had been held back for so long, almost against my better judgement I risked my all:

"It was said to you in ancient times: *'you shall not murder'*, and *'whoever murders* (even in rightful revenge) *shall be liable to judgement'*. But I say to you that if you are angry with a brother or sister you will be liable to judgement, and if you insult a brother or sister you will be liable to the council of the Sanhedrin, and if you accuse a brother or sister of rebelling against God you will be liable to the hell of fire."

But I say to you! With this one phrase I had just committed an act of schism. No longer satisfied by commenting on the Law, I was now making it. My fellow Pharisees would have happily agreed to an abstruse debate on the penal code of the Law, the legitimacy of the various jurisdictions in Israel, the quantum of sentences in proportion to the crime committed. There was no longer any doubt: by rebelling openly against the ancient tradition I myself had become a criminal, liable to judgement by the Sanhedrin.

Lost in a crowd of people to whom I had just promised happiness, they didn't respond, but from now on they would seek the slightest opportunity to make me talk about the Law.

And they would be lying in wait, following my every word.

26

Roused by this proclamation of a law of happiness, the crowd bore us along from village to village, from hillside to valley. They were intoxicated by the word I had used, "joyful", which was on everyone's lips; I just let them carry on. For such a long time they had thought that joy had ceased to exist! Having sensed the Pharisees' reticence, I was aware that happiness too makes demands, and that these go way beyond any commandments; that it isn't the ultimate aim and even less so the means to it, but a revolution in society's values. Whenever I tried to turn this promise into a reality I would come up against the different forces that compete for power in this country of ours. But at this early stage I just abandoned myself to the collective euphoria that was everywhere around us. I probably needed it, as did my disciples.

There followed a wonderful few weeks and months that I still remember as springtime in Galilee. The healings continued, sometimes several in swift succession. To get away from the crowds, my disciples suggested that we go across to the other side of the lake and spend a few days in the Decapolis. It would be my second trip into Gentile territory – but this time we wouldn't stay out of sight.

We had barely arrived when we came across one of those mentally deranged people who has been forced to leave his village because of his violent behaviour, and lives in caves or cemeteries. He threw himself at me – rarely had the Evil One, who was speaking with the voice of this man even more clearly than in the synagogue in Capernaum, manifested himself to me so overtly. Yet I knew that all I had to do was expose him, drive him out of the dark and dreadful recess where he lurks inside each and every one of us. The man was begging to be released from the jaws of the ravening beast; I simply had to bear witness to his wishes. He was healed immediately, but because they were terrified by what they saw as powerful magic, the Gentiles who lived there asked us to leave.

What I learnt from this was that only Jews have knowledge of the teaching of the prophets, the Psalms and the Book of Job, that they alone are aware that the Enemy exists. Misled by an array of different gods, convinced that all the misery in the world is simply a result of the indiscriminate workings of fate, Gentiles have too much faith in themselves. Unlike Jews, they don't have the inborn disquiet that is necessary in order to be reborn. I wouldn't speak to them in future, only to members of my own race.

When we got back to the Galilean side of the lake we were immediately surrounded by a large and boisterous crowd, which moved aside to allow a dignitary through. A Hellenized Jew, Jairus was a leader of the synagogue – so was he also about to tell me to move along? To my surprise he fell at my feet and begged me repeatedly:

"My little daughter is at the point of death. Come and lay your hands on her, so that she may be made well, and live!"

Tears in the wilderness… Suddenly, among the bustle of the crowd all I could see was this despairing father. I took him by the hand, and he got up and cleared a path through the mass of people who were crowding in from all sides. But in the midst of the uproar I suddenly stopped.

"Who touched my clothes?"

One of my disciples, I can't remember now which one, scoffed:
"You see the crowd pressing in on you; how can you say, 'Who touched me?'"

But I knew. A woman had come up behind me in the crowd and touched the hem of my coat. I turned round. Quite forgetting Jairus, again there was only one person among all the jostling, this trembling woman covered in dust. I bent down to her as if we were suddenly all alone in the world, and she told me she had been suffering from haemorrhages for many years. And so she had said to herself, "The rabbi whom everyone is talking about, perhaps..." I helped her to her feet.

"Daughter, your faith has made you well; go in peace, and be healed of your disease."

Even today I am still amazed by the razor-sharp acuity that I acquired during my struggle in the wilderness, which allows me instantly to discern another person's suffering. If I have ever had any kind of strength or power, then this is surely what it is. Rendered hypersensitive by my encounter with Evil, there is something deep inside me that is highly receptive, easily moved. Without realizing it, people who were sick in body and soul undoubtedly sensed this. What to me has always seemed miraculous is not the healing itself, but the convergence of the suffering that they are undergoing and the suffering I take upon myself, which Greek-speaking Jews refer to as *sympatheia*, or compassion.

In my teaching, this word would never take the place of "happiness". Buried deep within me, it would shake me to the core whenever I came across any kind of suffering.

A moment later, some people came from Jairus's house to say that his child was dead – there was no point in troubling the rabbi any further. I insisted on going back to his house with him, entering the room where the dead girl lay and taking her lifeless hand. By the time I left the house, she had got up and was walking about and eating. I strictly ordered the leader of the synagogue, the members of his family and his servants not to tell anyone about what had just taken place.

Like compassion, rebirth is buried deep within the mystery of God's creation.

27

I remember this period of time in the way dreams come back to us at the moment of waking: amid the haze, individual moments are as vivid as if we have actually experienced them. It was a whirl of healing and teaching, although the sequence of events is lost in the back roads of my mind. All that matters now is what remains of them, the feelings and convictions that are still strong.

Since people's minds seemed to be closed to parables I decided to stop using them for a while, and began teaching in maxims again, scattering them wherever I went.

Hillel once said: "If I am not for myself, then who will be?" Now I was a public figure, forever in view, I jealously guarded the time I spent on my own, when I was able to relive my experience in the wilderness, moments that were essentially *for me*. It was then that I gradually developed my ideas for the new Law. No longer afraid to be myself, I dared to get to the heart of the matter: I now felt ready to make a head-on assault on one of the bastions of Judaism.

"You have heard that it was said: '*An eye for an eye and a tooth for a tooth!*'"

The *lex talionis* is a permanent monument to our inability to understand each other, to see things from someone else's point of view, to look into the eyes of an adult and see the child that he or she once was. It perpetuates a primitive society based on hatred and inexpiable revenge passed down from generation to generation within a single family, neighbourhood or village.

"But I say to you, do not resist an evildoer. Quite the reverse…"

To allow yourself to be struck, stripped of your clothes, press-ganged without resisting is to overturn the Jewish Law, which lays down the means of redress available to the weak to protect them from the strong. This was going much further than any of the pagan philosophers, who teach self-mastery and indifference in the face of aggression. It was the first time that a doctrine of non-violent resistance had been propounded in Israel, but it was the only way to curb the fiery dance into which the Evil One leads us, chained together by the shackles of vengeance.

The Essenes had made this cast-iron rule even more inflexible. Any Jew who didn't follow the ways of their sect would no longer be regarded as their neighbour and brother, but as an opponent to be fought and destroyed. Alone in Israel, they openly preached hatred of one's fellow man, who was now the enemy. Without mentioning them by name (everyone would know whom I meant), I continued:

"You have heard that it was said: '*You shall love your neighbour and hate your enemy*.' But I say to you, love your enemies! For if you love only your brothers and sisters, what more are you doing than others?"

To love only those whose ideas, opinions and way of life we share is to legitimize the barriers set up by a sick and divided society, undermined by internecine conflicts. Among the crowd I noticed several people bristle – they had clearly spent time among the Essenes, whose view was that "those who are not with us are against us".

This was the first time I had broached the subject of boundaries, and it wouldn't be the last.

Yet still the Pharisees remained silent. After the death of John the Baptist, concerned to hear me challenging the laws of the Sabbath, they had been circumspect in their questioning – did I still regard myself as a practising Jew? I left them in no doubt about where my loyalties lay: disputing the way a commandment is enforced isn't the same as declaring it invalid. And yet now...

"Again, you have heard that it was said to those of ancient times: *'You shall not swear falsely, but carry out the vows you have made to the Lord.'"*

They pricked up their ears. In Israel, the practice of oath-taking forms the basis of daily life. In a world riddled with envy, malice and conflicting interests, how was it possible to know who was telling the truth and who was lying? Since it involved God as a witness and third party, an oath taken in his name guaranteed that a claim or testimony was true, meaning that an innocent person would not be punished, a shopkeeper would be paid and a creditor would get what he was owed. But the One I found in the wilderness couldn't be used to serve human interests in this way.

"But I say to you: *Do not swear at all!* Neither by heaven, for it is the throne of God, nor by the earth, for it is his footstool."

By abolishing the age-old use of oaths, it was the first time I hadn't simply modified the Law – I was now revoking it, there was no other word for it. I was claiming that human relationships should be based on mutual trust and respect, not Divine authority. God is in heaven – but here on earth it is for us to establish a civil society that is worthy of him, not justify our actions by having recourse to his authority.

To do this was to announce the end of theocracy in Israel. I ought to have been arrested on the spot. I think it was only the atmosphere of popular euphoria in which I lived and worked that prevented disciplinary action being taken – although not their feelings of resentment.

These weren't shared by all of the Pharisees, among whom there were naturally differences. Some of them were still well disposed towards me, even invited me to meals in their homes. These I felt I could trust.

During one of these suppers there was an incident that still fills me with a comforting glow whenever I think of it, even now. It was a quite formal occasion, we were reclining on couches round a table in the middle of the room. Then in came a woman without any head covering, whose long, flowing hair advertised the fact that she was a prostitute. In the silence that promptly descended, this woman, whose very touch would make you unclean, and simply *ought not to have been there*, slipped past the other guests and took an alabaster flask from the front of her low-cut dress. I felt her hot tears on my feet, her hair drying them, the brush of her lips. The room was filled with the strong smell of perfume – she had her hands on me, she was massaging my ankles! My host sat speechless, eyes bulging. This creature had dared venture out of the gutter where some of those round the table sometimes went to call on her, safe in the knowledge that the wall of opprobrium that surrounded her would safeguard them and their reputations. By touching this unseeing, oblivious rabbi, not only was she sullying him, but also the pillars of society who were gathered here; she might even recognize one or two of her occasional clients, she had to be dispatched whence she came or there might be a scandal.

Not once had the woman spoken. I looked deep into her eyes, listened to what they were saying: all I am able to do is love, they said, to make you understand this I am using the tools of my trade, my untied hair, my sweet, gentle lips, the perfume that men find so enticing, my caresses. But what of my tears of anguish! O Rabbi, tell me that your God will not condemn someone for the crime of love!

I turned to the Pharisee:

"Simon, I have something to say to you."

"Master," he replied, "speak."

Because she had so much ground to catch up, this woman had run the distance in an instant. The only way she was able to express her thoughts and feelings was by these actions; it was for me to tell her that love had the power to release her from the clutches of Evil, that no fall is permanent or beyond God's sphere of influence. By entering this house she had proved that she believed in forgiveness, thus overcoming the barriers of shame and ignominy. In the same way, her faith would help her to be reborn. From this day forward she would live and love quite differently – the Pharisee and his dinner guests needed to hear this as much as she did.

"Because of what she has just done, I tell you that her sins, which were many, have been forgiven; for she has shown great love."

Then I said to her:

"Your sins are forgiven, your faith has saved you, go in peace."

There were two occasions when a woman gazed into my eyes – this one now, and another that came later – and both will be imprinted on my memory for ever. Even if I failed as a prophet, even if I was unable to help Israel fulfil its destiny, perhaps these two gazes alone might mean that my life wasn't lived in vain. Tonight, I can still feel her eyes burning into me like divine love.

28

My words heard by crowds of people, acclaimed wherever I went, leaving a trail of healings behind me, having questioned the enforcement of several laws and abolished one of them without suffering any consequences – it was a time when I truly believed that I could do anything. I was offering Israel the opportunity to be reborn, and this nation whose joints had seized up over the years was going to take hold of it with both hands, regain the prophetic spirit of its youth, bend the knee before God once more. I could, I should set up a popular movement. I had to expand my activities, become a permanent presence in Galilee – I had to involve the Twelve.

All they had done so far was to follow me obediently everywhere; calling themselves my disciples was a delusion. If I was able to tell when people were sick in body and soul, detect how far some of them had come already, if I could help them to their feet, then why couldn't Peter, Andrew, James, John and the others do the same? Every minute of the day, hadn't they witnessed the tide of compassion that flowed out from me to those who were shackled by Evil, sweeping away the barriers that stood between us? Although not close, was the fellowship we shared not strong enough for them to play a part in my campaign of renewal?

I had to try at least. So I decided to send them out into the surrounding villages, in the same way the Essenes travelled the countryside; like them they would go out two by two, taking nothing for their journey – no bread, no bag, no money in their belts, no spare clothes. Yet unlike the people from Qumran, who are only allowed to stay with members of their sect, they would rely on traditional Jewish hospitality, lodging wherever they were offered accommodation. Remembering what had happened in the Decapolis, I simply told them:

"Greet no Gentiles on the road. Go rather to the lost sheep of the house of Israel."

Just like they had seen me do, they would bear witness to the healing of the sick. But should their actions be followed up by words, as mine were? Were they able to teach? I had only given them a vague outline of the new law, and knew they hadn't grasped the full implications of the word "joyful". So I told them to confine themselves to the Baptist's teaching: "You must be converted!" Yes, they were probably capable of that.

Meanwhile, I would go away to a deserted place.

To drink deeply from the wellspring of silence. And see Satan fall from heaven.

When they got back they were in seventh heaven. As my followers they had been welcomed everywhere as messengers from On-High. My reputation, the stories they told about my healings had turned people's heads – particularly their own. They had taken on the mantle of Elijah without having paid the price in tears, and if the sick felt better after meeting them, then they took sole credit for the healing.

Cracks began to appear in my rosy optimism. Would I be able to convey the sense of Awakening to them, they who hadn't experienced the torment of the wilderness like I had?

Without offering any explanation, I commanded them to get into the boat and come away to a deserted place by themselves. What they needed was solitude, so they too could drink at the well of silence.

But it was now impossible for us to go anywhere without being noticed. No sooner had we come ashore than we were surrounded by crowds of people who had hurried there on foot from the neighbouring villages. Oh, but now it wasn't Pharisees come to savour the delights of a debate, or wealthy dinner guests fed on honours and distinctions, but a distraught and wild-eyed flock, the people of Israel wandering around like sheep without a shepherd. At the sight of these people abandoned to their despair, I was shaken to the core. They were the same ones whose harrowing existence I had promised totally to transform. Once more I spoke to them of justice and forgiveness, of peace and sharing with others – in a word, about happiness, which up till now I had used as a ploughshare to carve out a brand-new furrow.

Dusk fell quickly. My disciples came to me and said:

"This is a deserted place, and the hour is now very late... If you send them away hungry they might faint on the way, and some of them have come a great distance!"

As I have already mentioned, from the start of our itinerant life, whenever we found ourselves in an isolated spot our benefactors would send whatever food we needed. I glanced round: the crowd was quite large and becoming restless; then among the toing and froing I saw a small train of mules arrive, laden with baskets filled to the brim with bread and dried fish. People had seen me cross the lake, seen the crowd gathering.

By people, I mean the wives of our patrons. Once again they were there when they were needed.

I asked everyone to sit on the grass, helped my disciples unload the mules then told them to share out the food:

"You give them something to eat."

As they walked through the crowd, hands stretched out from every side towards the bulging baskets. Among the confusion no one had noticed the provisions arriving or me taking charge of them, but they could all see the outcome – as much food as they could eat! Cries of wild excitement ran through the crowd, which were soon taken up by my companions – the rabbi had produced all this from a few loaves, as the Prophet Elisha had done with the bread and oil. A miracle! It was a miracle!

A *miracle*... Their desire for marvels prevented them from understanding what had happened, which to me was the very image of what I expected to see in the new Israel: wealthy benefactors ensuring the needs of the poor were taken care of, voluntarily sharing their food with them, and then this impromptu supper on the grass, evocative of another feast – the one we will all eventually partake in in God's presence on the day when social differences no longer exist!

But by now no one was listening to me – they all wolfed down their portion then set off for home. I would have rebuked my disciples for not quelling this insane rumour and allowing the crowd to believe it was a miracle, but my strength and courage failed me.

I told them to pick up what was left, which was scattered over the grass. They gathered up far more bread and fish than our small group were able to eat – so they filled several baskets with what remained and sent it back to the people who had so generously provided it.

Overcome by great weariness, I watched the mule train leave.

If only these disciples, whose hearts were hardened by delusions of grandeur, would go home too! I told them to get back into the boat and go on ahead of me to Bethsaida, where some of them lived. Telling them that I preferred to walk, I said I would go round the shore and catch up with them later.

But as soon as they had hoisted the tiny sail, I headed away from the lake. Tonight was for me alone, the mountain my sole refuge and witness.

29

There were several subsequent occasions when, disheartened by the Twelve's attitude, I decided to spend the night praying on my own. This was highly unusual for a Jew, for whom prayer involves addressing God in public – generally by chanting the eighteen Ritual Blessings, which only takes about forty-five minutes. So what did this rabbi of theirs do by himself for the whole night?

They couldn't understand. How could I describe the process of slowly entering deep into the silence, stripping everything away until the mind is empty of thoughts, and you stand face to face with a Presence that words cannot describe and which is beyond physical perception, yet whose reality gradually exerts its influence, seemingly of its own accord? No: during these long nights I never spoke, not even inwardly. Would I fill the void that divided me from God with chatter? Give him a detailed account of my various moods? He knew everything, without me having to utter a word.

I listened. I calmed and quieted my soul. It was inside me like a little child, a weaned child with its mother.

Who was it who decided that God is male? The Jews have always seen him as a grave-faced patriarch who rules over Israel, the father of the nation, the father of the king, the father of each and every one of us. Yet in the soothing peace of the night I discovered a loving side to him, like a mother suckling her child.

God the father? This was also God the mother, bending over me, surrounding me with sweet, boundless love.

Legendary figures would sometimes appear before my mind's eye, men such as Elijah or Moses, whose epic tale provides some of the most beautiful passages in the Law. All Jews revere them, yet no one ever dreams of identifying with them – but in these nights of breathtaking silence I came to realize that I was destined to live my life as a continuation of theirs. Like Elijah, I would be hounded by priests and tyrants. Like Moses, a burning bush would refuse to tell me its name so I could come to know God's fatherly affection and create a new name for this relationship, something that was unheard of in Israel. And, like Moses and Elijah, I would live and die alone, face to face with the One God.

The next morning something happened that would fill me with self-doubt, as well as shattering my illusions about my disciples.

I found them in the midst of a large gathering for whom they were the centre of attention, arguing with some Scribes. As soon as people saw me they rushed over and overwhelmed me with boisterous greetings. So what had happened in my absence?

I questioned the Twelve:

"What are you arguing about with them?"

A man came forward, holding the hand of a young boy with a blank expression on his face.

"Rabbi, I brought you my son. He has a spirit that makes him unable to speak, and whenever it seizes him, it dashes him down, and he foams at the mouth and grinds his teeth and becomes rigid."

It wasn't unusual to come across people afflicted with this strange malady, which would unexpectedly throw them to the ground, foaming at the mouth, the whites of their eyes showing. Since the doctors seemed unable to do anything to help them, superstition had the last word: these people were possessed by one of the spirits that inhabit the Jewish subconscious. Having exhausted all other possibilities, the father had come to the rabbi of whom people spoke so highly – but in his absence...

"I asked your disciples to cast out the spirit, but they could not do so."

So that was it! Their conquest of the crowds had gone to my followers' heads, and they had decided to show off their newfound abilities. No sooner had they begun to have faith than they believed they possessed magic powers. Left to themselves they had wanted to produce evidence of these, convince the Scribes, perform healings like I did, take my place – hence succumbing to conventional beliefs, they who had never set foot in the arena to do battle with the true enemy, the Evil One... Faced with such prosaic gullibility I couldn't contain my anger:

"You faithless generation, how much longer must I be among you? How much longer must I put up with you? Bring him to me!"

As he was brought over he had a fit and fell to the ground, seized with convulsions, rolling about and foaming at the mouth. I asked his father how long this had been happening, and he said that the boy, now a youth, had had it since childhood, that the spirit sometimes cast him into fire or water to kill him. In a voice bereft of hope he cried out:

"If you can do anything, have pity on us and help us!"

If you can... The man was questioning my self-belief, perhaps even my faith in God. For a moment I hesitated: God? Not once had I doubted him. But myself? Here, in front of my dull-witted disciples, all these wide-eyed people, the sceptical Scribes, not to mention the brutal presence of Evil and all this anguish, would I be capable of manifesting my faith in his son's ability to be reborn? I tried to overcome my doubts:

"*If you can!* Everything is possible for him who believes."

Immediately the father of the child cried out: "I believe; help my unbelief!"

Never had I been so acutely conscious of the secret resilience of the Jewish people, the deep-seated relationship between its poorest, most humble members and the mystery of the Invisible as I was at that moment. This simple man had travelled much further into the depths of faith than I had. He was asking me to leave my hesitation behind, to stand beside him on the other side of doubt. Driven into a corner, the father of this boy was demanding that I act like a prophet.

Bending down, I took the boy by the hand and lifted him up. Immediately his eyes brightened, he started breathing normally, he wiped his mouth and smiled at me.

On the way back to their village, my disciples walked along without speaking, their eyes fixed on the ground in front of them. Eventually they asked me, shamefacedly:

"So… why could we not cast out this spirit?"

"Do you still not perceive or understand? Are your hearts hardened?"

There was no point. As if talking to myself I just added:

"This kind… can come out only through prayer."

Unable to utter another word, I suddenly felt the need to go back to the solitude of the Judaean desert, where everything had begun. But events would conspire against me.

30

While my popularity with the crowds didn't go unnoticed in Galilee, word also spread beyond the region itself. A delegation who had been sent from Jerusalem with the express intention of finding me were able to do so without any difficulty. When I saw them coming I realized things were getting serious – because this time it was senior Pharisees, along with more Scribes.

I invited them to eat with us. Without even sitting down they set about interrogating me:

"Why do your disciples not adhere to the ancient tradition and eat with defiled hands?"

They clearly hadn't come all this way just to find out if my disciples washed their hands before eating. In any case, I knew that very few Pharisees set store by this ritual requirement, and that like most ordinary Jews my disciples often neglected to do it. No, their sole concern was my teaching on the Law. For the sake of some theoretical state of happiness, had I decided to free myself from the commandments, both major and minor, once and for all? If I had replaced the tradition with an ill-defined, idealistic notion of beatitude, could I still be considered a Jewish rabbi?

Such a serious matter had to be resolved between fellow Pharisees; they would never dream of broaching the subject with laymen present. While they were vacillating, I decided to clear the air:

"You abandon the commandment of God and hold to human tradition!"

The crowd listened closely to every word of this fraught exchange, which went against every Pharisaic custom. The time for tact and diplomacy was well and truly over! I reminded them of Moses's fifth commandment, which sets children helping their elderly parents above all else. Then I accused them of shamefully perverting this law, by giving sons permission to keep the goods that they were legally bound to use to support their mother and father:

"Hypocrites! You make void the word of God through your tradition that you have handed on!"

The whispering among the crowd was a sign that what I said was true. The ordinary working people, who set great store by showing respect for elderly relatives, were unhappy about exemptions from the Law such as these. So were the dignitaries quibbling? I would show them that I was no anarchist who just opposed the Law as a matter of principle. The path to happiness demands sacrifices too, but it was the very foundation of the Law that I was planning to change.

Calling the crowd over, I spoke to them over the Pharisees' heads:

"Listen to me, all of you, and understand: there is nothing outside a person that by going in can defile, but the things that come out are what defile!"

A murmur of uncertainty ran through the crowd: what was the rabbi getting at? What did this have to do with the question? Was I daring to announce that all foods were pure?

Offended at being accused of hypocrisy, the worthies promptly turned their backs on me and walked away, followed by some of the people. My disciples gathered round, confused.

"Then do you also fail to understand?"

Whatever goes into a person from outside cannot defile them, because it is only passing through. What debases and destroys a person comes from deep within them – the thoughts that give rise to wounding words, which cause others to respond with malicious deeds. I explained the vicious circle of thoughts-words-deeds. It wasn't the end result of this circle that we had to tackle, by imposing one rule after another, but the origin of it, the thoughts that come from our hearts. Our heart is a source of good as well as Evil. It is in a person's heart that their fate is decided.

The law of the heart! I had found the lodestar of my teaching, the key to the happiness that I promised. It wasn't just a person's hands or the rest of their body that had to be cleansed, but what lies within.

They had to correct their desires, not create more rules.

To be quite certain that they understood, I made my point clear: purifying the heart doesn't mean that we are allowed to do whatever we like, that there is total freedom. Quite the reverse, it introduced a universal law that made far more demands than the Jewish Law – because it didn't simply assess people's behaviour, it got to the very root of it.

If my disciples were to grasp the revolutionary nature of what I was suggesting, they would have to join me in my long nights of inner prayer. It was in this crucible that I had discovered the vital role played by thoughts, and then gradually located the place where they originate.

The Pharisees in Jerusalem had just forced me to articulate the law that went hand in hand with my Beatitudes. From now on my teaching could be summed up in two words that complemented each other: *joyful* and *heart*. I realized that this wouldn't please those in high places. To replace the Law with a greater but unverifiable authority would undermine their position as judges, as well as the power that goes with it. No one could be expected to govern a country on the basis of its people's state of inner purity: they weren't mystics, they were rulers – and they would be the first to suffer the consequences of my teaching.

It was almost the Passover, the second since I had begun my life of wandering. But before going back to Jerusalem I thought it wise to keep out of sight for a while, so I went over the border to the north and into Gentile territory.

31

What was once the land of the Phoenicians is now part of the Empire's Syrian province. The population is more mixed than in Palestine, and they speak the same Aramaic from which ours originates, although theirs is corrupted by Greek – the official language used by virtually everyone.

There are many wealthy Jewish merchants living there, who make their money from the trade between Tyr, Sidon and the Mediterranean Basin. They mixed in the same circles as my rich clients in Sepphoris, and like them were always hospitable to me. Whenever I went to their homes I advised them not to tell anyone that I was there – after the commotion by the lake and the clash with the Pharisees from Jerusalem I needed peace and quiet. Not only that, we were surrounded by Gentiles, people whom Jews avoid. But despite our efforts the rumour mill was still working, and it was almost impossible for me and my troop of disciples to go unnoticed.

So it was that a Syrian woman came to the house. As soon as she saw me she threw herself at my feet, and begged me in Aramaic interspersed with Greek to heal her daughter, whom she had left at home. I was startled: did she really think that I would go to a Gentile house, thus making myself unclean? Did she take me for one of the quack doctors who hired themselves out? I remembered what I had resolved after healing the deranged man in the Decapolis: it had occurred to me at that point that rebirth was meant for Jews alone, not for Gentiles. I told her this quite plainly: I had been sent only to the lost sheep of the house of Israel.

Hearing her moans, my disciples gathered round, all agreeing with me: as a Jew, their rabbi should concern himself solely with Jews, the only people who had a covenant with God. But the woman kept begging, her voice grew louder and louder. Now annoyed, they started muttering among themselves that she ought to be sent away, back to the darkness of her pagan beliefs. To put an end to it I snapped at her:

"It is not fair to take the children's food and throw it to the dogs."

To make myself perfectly clear, I used the word *kynarion*, or "little dog", an insult in vernacular Greek that Jews are familiar with because they use it as a way of expressing their contempt for Gentiles. To my surprise she didn't retaliate, but just looked up at me, her face bathed in tears. I will never forget what she said; it still echoes in my mind tonight because it changed my life completely:

"Yes, but even the dogs under the table eat their masters' crumbs!"

I was speechless with shock. Yet again a woman had shattered my male Jewish preconceptions! The Samaritan woman at the well had made me realize that I had to go back to the very source of the Ten Commandments, that by formalizing them Moses had limited people's contact with God. And now this Gentile was telling me that God is the same for everyone, that he doesn't have a covenant with one specific nation, but that his compassion extends throughout the world!

And that she was ready to receive this gift from me.

I can't remember what I said to her. Her faith was more genuine than that of any Jew whom I had healed; she had beaten me.

Nothing could withstand that: so when she got home she would find that her daughter was healed.

All this left me gasping for breath. As a Jew I had been brought up to believe that my people had been chosen as the stewards of a Law that was more perfect than any other. I had now begun to look more deeply into this Law, to go beyond its bounds, but was I willing to stretch it to its limit, make it extend to the whole world? God was God for everyone, of course. But was the One God of Israel as much the father of the Gentiles as he was of the Jews?

If that was true... then what of me? Did I stand in the long line of Jewish prophets, continuing their work, fulfilling the message that they had addressed to the people of Israel alone... or would this fulfilment now take on a more all-embracing dimension, one I had never considered?

Who was I? *Who am I?*

I set these questions aside until later – if we were going to be in Jerusalem in time for the Passover, we had to set off immediately. I decided to go along the left bank of the Jordan and stay in Gentile territory. Still in a state of shock, I didn't feel able to face the Pharisees and crowds of Jews in Galilee. Surprised to see me so troubled, my disciples walked either side of me without speaking.

Ever since we left the Jordan, I hadn't had a chance to talk to them at length. Permanently surrounded by crowds thirsting for miracles, increasingly under observation by the authorities, just having them with me was enough. They were able to see, hear and scrutinize everything I said and did. When I left John the Baptist I didn't have a particular plan in mind, it was only gradually, during the course of my various encounters, that I became aware how unique my message was. But them? Knowing their background, I suspected that their motives (especially those of the former activists) were likely to be mainly political – to drive out the Roman occupiers, seize power and create a position for themselves. So they must have also been wondering, not only what part I played in Jewish society, but who I really was.

When we stopped for a rest, I decided that I had to be clear in my mind about this, so I asked them: "What do people say about me? Who do they think I am?"

Their answer was an indication of their state of confusion:

"For some you are John the Baptist. For others, Elijah, and for others still, one of the prophets who has returned from the dead…"

This was no surprise. For some unknown reason, despite centuries of official teaching the ordinary Jewish people still hold to their irrational belief in a form of reincarnation, which serves to allay their fear of death more than the doctrine of resurrection expounded by the Pharisees. The fact that people were saying that the headless John the Baptist, or one of the prophets of old, lived on in me didn't surprise me in the least. But those who had known the Baptist, who had been with me constantly since I had moved on from his teaching, what did they really think? I had to know.

It was Peter who stepped forward:

"You are the Messiah!"

So that was it! John the Baptist, Elijah and Jeremiah had only been prophets, they had never harboured political ambitions. The Jewish people, on the other hand, were consumed with the idea of the coming Messiah, who would lead them in wresting back power from the Gentiles and restoring the Kingdom of David. Hadn't the Zealots' idol, Judas of Galilee, declared himself to be the Messiah at the beginning of the century, before embarking on a Jewish rebellion that would end in a fruitless bloodbath? We had been living together for over a year – didn't the dazzling sight of the crowds that gathered round me fuel the fervent messianic dreams of the Barjona, the Boanerges brothers and Iscariot?

But when they eventually realized that I had no intention of leading any kind of liberation movement, would they desert me? Or worse, would they slip away and join the ranks of my opponents?

You are the Messiah! I sternly ordered them never to refer to me as the *Messiah* – never, not to anyone! And I reminded them that the prophets had all been persecuted. If I continued to follow the call of the wilderness then I couldn't expect to be crowned as a political Messiah, but to suffer the same fate as those who came before me, to be subjected to physical pain.

Peter's reaction was as stern as my warning to them. He took me aside and began to rebuke me: yes, maybe other people had failed, but you won't, please God you won't! The healings, the ecstatic crowds, a teaching that even unsettled the authorities in Jerusalem... Was I going to give all that up because of some fanciful notion that I had been called to suffer? Didn't that mean I was just a damp squib?

All of a sudden it was as if I was back in the wilderness, face to face with the Enemy who had done everything in his power to turn me away from the path I had to follow. The Evil One was putting words into Peter's mouth in order to tempt me again, to try and destroy me by holding out the promise of worldly power. Drawing myself up, I turned to him and exclaimed, as forcefully as before:

"Get behind me, Satan!"

I thought he would pack up and leave immediately, bitterly offended by this insult – the worst that any Jew could direct at another – taking the Eleven with him. But, perhaps in thrall to my authority, he just hung his head and went back to the others, who hadn't moved from where they were standing.

But from then on as we travelled the length and breadth of Galilee or Judaea, they didn't walk at my side as they had before. They followed behind in a small group, talking among themselves – leaving me to go on ahead by myself, taking them along a road that led they knew not where.

32

The sight of Jerusalem brought me little joy. The Judaean came to meet me and urged me to be careful: since the events in Galilee, some of the Pharisees – those who opposed me – had made formal complaints to the Sanhedrin. My friend, a fellow Nazarene who like me no longer offered sacrifices in the Temple, made me promise not to put in an appearance on the esplanade, which was where all the debates, as well as all the trouble, took place. I would be able to have some peace and quiet at Lazarus's house in Bethany.

Knowing I was there, the women who supported us practically or financially came to see me nearly every day. There were wealthy Galileans or dignitaries' wives such as Joanna, who was married to Chuza (Herod's steward), all of them under the leadership of someone called Mary – who had vowed me her undying gratitude ever since I had healed her of a host of different ailments in Magdala, her home village. Mary Magdalene was one of those who would sometimes come with us from town to town, organizing our food and accommodation with total disregard for what people might say. These women were open to my teaching in a way that my disciples and men in general were not. They were especially eager to hear parables, and I gladly started using these realistic allegories again in order to tell them about rebirth and inner purity.

They would listen avidly – as wives and mothers, the law of the heart struck a chord with them.

One day, Martha burst into the room. Seeing her sister Mary sitting at my feet, drinking in my words, she rebuked me: with so many guests in the house, didn't I care that she had been left to wait on everyone and prepare all the parts of the meal? With a smile I told her not to be so worried and distracted by things: by listening to me, Mary had chosen the better part, which could not be taken away from her.

Nicodemus also came to see me, bringing a man called Joseph, who was from the Jewish village of Arimathea, and who like him was a member of the Sanhedrin. They confirmed what the Judaean feared: people in high places were troubled by my behaviour. Yet individual Pharisees within the Council had differing opinions: Hillel's disciples preferred to allow a colleague to interpret the Law as he wished, while those who followed Shammai were outraged by what they saw as my liberal approach. As for the Sadducees, as long as I wasn't critical of the Temple and its form of worship and didn't cause trouble in Jerusalem, unrest in far-off Galilee was of little interest to them.

Nicodemus made me promise to follow our friend the Judaean's advice, and not draw attention to myself while I was in Jerusalem.

So I took to spending part of the night in the Garden of Gethsemane, which played its part by being dark and deserted. On the other side of the Kidron Valley, the great walls of the Temple were bathed in spring moonlight just as they are tonight. I could hear the murmur of the festive crowds quite clearly, and gave myself up to memories of my childhood.

Ever since the Law was handed down to Moses on Mount Sinai, the Jews have stopped asking questions about God. Petrified at the thought of the Last Judgement, they regard this all-powerful and distant lawmaker as the supreme arbiter. Yet in their oracles, for a long time the prophets have painted a quite different picture of God, that of a deeply compassionate father who is moved and even distressed by his children's suffering.

Steeped in a Mediterranean culture where the father figure has the power of life and death over his family, haunted by fear of the Law, the Jews have eventually lost sight of God's other side, which the prophets describe in such a circumspect way. During my long nights of solitary prayer, it was to him, father and mother at once, that I opened my heart.

In the presence of God's loving kindness, I saw how vital it was to return to childhood, the childhood of hearts and minds.

During my first year of travelling in Galilee, having left the fear and trembling proclaimed by John the Baptist behind, I had made happiness the ethos of a new law, a breath of fresh air with which I invited the Jews to fill their lungs. But now I had to go further, demonstrate that they would only achieve this happiness by totally transforming their everyday relationship with God. A child wasn't merely that unfinished human being who was looked down on throughout the Roman Empire, and who was worth nothing – in fact who didn't exist until he or she reached adulthood.

I began to see that this new law would have unforeseen consequences: to attain God's plenitude, people would have to change, become like little children again.

In my Kingdom, the child was the young prince.

I celebrated the Passover at Lazarus's house, carving and sharing the paschal lamb with his neighbours at nightfall, as was customary. The grandeur of the age-old rituals, the sumptuously laden table lit by the menorah, the baskets of unleavened bread, the plates of bitter herbs, the traditional dialogue between the father and son, the two cups of wine passed round among the members of the assembled family, the singing of Psalms, all this filled me with boundless delight…

I didn't realize it at the time, but this would probably be my last Passover.

At dawn the next day, the beginning of the week, we set off back to Galilee.

33

The memories of my second year of teaching are still buzzing around inside my head. The people of Galilee were overjoyed to see me again. Often I found myself surrounded, almost crushed by the crowds. On more than one occasion I had to ask my disciples to keep a boat ready, so I could stand in it and still be heard by the vast numbers who gathered on the shore to listen with an enjoyment that was plain to see.

When I first began preaching, still in awe of John the Baptist, I had tried to put Hillel's words into practice: "If I am not *for myself*, then who will be?" Now free to be myself quite unrestrainedly, I remembered what he had also said: "But if I am *only for myself*, then who am I?"

I no longer existed for myself, but for them. A prophet's life is not his own, it belongs to the people among whom he was born, from whom he distances himself only in order to draw closer to them. I have never sought fame, nor to be loved for myself, yet I felt a deep emotional attachment to these destitute people, a feeling they heartily reciprocated.

The reaction of those who came to listen to me at Lazarus's house prompted me to start teaching in parables again. What did it matter if I wasn't understood by priests locked away inside entrenched opinions, or by self-important disciples! I knew the common people would hear me, because I spoke their language.

I must admit that the hostility shown towards my earliest teaching by a section of the Pharisees wasn't wholly unfounded. Inner purity is a private, individual matter; my Beatitudes and the law of the heart now had to enter the public domain, the community outside of which no Jew can reach an understanding of himself or apprehend what destiny holds for him.

During the course of my different healings, it occurred to me that rebirth is a form of new creation: the young man in Nain, Jairus's daughter, the paralytic at the pool in Beth-zatha, the repentant prostitute... after meeting me, these people would never be the same again. Being healed had brought a new order to their lives.

I had to draw attention to the connection between rebirth and divine creation. The Jewish Law holds that God the Creator is the supreme ruler of the world, which he created out of nothing. So rebirth could only mean taking your place in a universe that was under the sway of God's kingship. Yet the phrase *Kingdom of God* or *Kingdom of Heaven* doesn't appear anywhere in the sacred texts: to say that God is the ruler of his creation (and of Israel) is one thing, but claiming that a "Kingdom of God" exists somewhere is quite another. Ever since the Jewish people became dispersed, the word *kingdom* has acquired political overtones, a whiff of restoration that sustains the desire for rebellion that lies buried inside every Jew.

Was I empathizing with the mostly ill-defined longings of these people in order to be better understood by them? I began referring to the happiness I promised them as the "coming of the Kingdom of God". I thought that all I needed to do was fill this empty shell, this rarely used expression, with something completely unequivocal that couldn't be appropriated for political purposes.

If I keep watch tonight, waiting for the end to come, it could be that in making this choice I assumed that the people around me were capable of understanding what my intentions were.

This Kingdom had to become part of everyday life for the Jewish people. In Israel, the tradition of mealtimes is one that breathes life into the community. The sumptuous food, the copious quantities of wine are an excuse to enjoy each other's company, a group of individuals who are very different from one another yet who are brought together by table fellowship. A momentary happiness, yes, but the very real one of taking our rightful place at a banquet where the host accords each guest his share of food and honour, so no one feels forgotten or ignored.

I began by telling the story of the king who gave a banquet to celebrate the marriage of his son, and sent his servants to call those who had been invited. Or the bridegroom who asked his friends to stand outside the room where the wedding feast was taking place, holding lamps to light the way for the guests... but what if the king's guests refused to come? Or the bridegroom's friends let their lamps go out before the guests arrived?

What they lacked in education, my listeners made up for with sound common sense. For them, their wedding day was a once-in-a-lifetime event for which they had burdened themselves with enormous debts so as to make it a special occasion. In that case, they replied, if the guests won't come, the king should invite anyone to the feast, even people who happen to be walking past! As for the friends of the bridegroom who let their lamps go out, they should be made to stay outside the banqueting hall while the couple celebrate inside!

I went on: the Kingdom of God is like a field where a farmer accidentally unearths a chest full of gold while he is ploughing. He immediately hurries off and sells all he owns so he can buy the field. Viewed in another way, it's a form of mortgage on the future, like sowing seed. The farmers sow the seed then gather in ripe grain and couch grass alike. It's only afterwards (when it's too late) that they separate the good from the bad and burn the weeds.

I wanted them to understand that to enter the Kingdom is to turn your back on the past and embark on a different venture, that of a new way of life. The law of the heart involves a gamble. You know what you are leaving behind, but not what lies ahead, or whether you will find it equally satisfying. Not only that, we live in a world where everything is mixed together, the good with the bad. For if the Kingdom promises harmony, this world brings only discord and confrontation.

My parables opened up old wounds among my audience. There was one question that they asked incessantly – *when* will we see this Kingdom? As John the Baptist had done, I said that it was nigh, that the time was fast approaching. But *when*, they exhorted me? Will it be soon, how much longer must we wait? They were so impatient, filled with such despair, such yearning for change that I eventually said:

"There are some standing here who will not taste death until they see that the Kingdom of God has come with power."

So it would come to this generation! When I saw how excited this made them I realized I might have gone too far. But their elation was such that there was no going back. So I tried to qualify these parables by telling others: the Kingdom of God is like yeast mixed in with the dough, it takes all night to make it rise! Or a single seed that someone sows in a field and which eventually, but much later, grows into a great tree where the birds of the air make nests in its branches. I wanted them to realize that the timescale of the Kingdom is not the same as our own. In his lifetime, none of the prophets saw the seeds he sowed grow into ears of ripe corn rippling in the breeze.

So, was the end of the world imminent, would it come soon or later? I would pay a high price for the ambivalent replies I gave them.

After a long period of travelling punctuated by teaching, we made our way along the lake to Capernaum. As was now usual, I went on ahead by myself. Behind me my disciples were engaged in a vigorous discussion, snatches of which reached me on the breeze.

When we got to the town, I turned round and asked them:

"What were you arguing about on the way?"

Clearly embarrassed, at first they wouldn't tell me. Eventually they admitted that throughout the journey they had been arguing about which of them was the greatest. I was so astonished that I had to sit down. So when I said "Kingdom", they had taken this to mean "power"! From all my parables, the only thing that stuck in their minds was that they would see the Kingdom of God come with power *in their lifetime*. To them, this meant I had committed myself to restoring a Jewish state straight away, that they would share the spoils. Weren't my healings an enduring sign of my strength? The people were with me, power was within my grasp. And besides, why would I have singled them out as the Twelve if I weren't planning to appoint each of them as the head of one of the twelve tribes of Israel, this fragmented nation that would rebuild itself under my kingship?

These few scanty facts preoccupied their overworked minds. Among the whirlwind that raged inside their heads, one question stood out: which of them would sit at my right hand, take the place of honour?

There wasn't only a lack of understanding between us, but a yawning abyss. After all these months I still hadn't managed to get my message across! I called over a little child who was walking past and stood him in the middle of these Twelve pretenders to the throne.

"Whoever among you wants to be first must be last of all and servant of all."

But their God was the God of the Messiah, and the only kingdom they were capable of conceiving was that of a Messiah, in other words a political kingdom. While for me, this child who was toddling around in front of us was the very image of what I wanted to be in God's eyes. Without another word I ruffled his hair and sent him back to his games.

The Twelve and I no longer had the same God.

We continued to travel together, me leading the way. But we were no longer on the same road.

34

This incident proved that the most politically aware among my listeners were reflecting on the nature of the Kingdom of God as much as on the moment when it would come. To the former Essenes it meant the end of a corrupt clergy who were leading Israel into darkness. For the devotees of Zealot violence it would bring a drastic change in Jewish society in both social and political terms. But for all the factions there would first be an armed revolt for which they had to prepare themselves, followed by a great bloodletting.

The Pharisees in Galilee, meanwhile, had managed to decipher my parables without any difficulty. The Kingdom was the Jewish people, who had been invited to a feast and were gathered together round the host in happiness. This host (or this king), was the One God of Israel. Like at all banquets there would be a seating plan, a structure – and this was the Law. Even if the metaphors I used seemed unorthodox to them, they didn't depart completely from the prophetic tradition, so the Pharisees could bear with them. But they raised one major question that refused to go away, regarding the frontiers of this new Kingdom. Exactly *who* would be invited to this banquet? *Who* would be allowed into the room where the marriage feast was held? Only Jews, or would there be Gentiles too? Or... was I suggesting that the Gentiles would eventually take the Jews' place, as my parable about the king seemed to imply?

This, I sensed, was the perennial concern of those whose role it was to safeguard the identity of the Jewish people. If we still existed, it was because we had built a wall between ourselves and everyone else – namely, the Law of Moses. It was an invisible wall that wound its way from northern Galilee to the south of Judaea, and which every Jew in the Diaspora carried within him, a place of shelter where he could continue to be a Jew even if he wasn't in Israel. So was the rabbi saying that one day God would demolish this wall and allow anyone into the citadel of his Kingdom?

The Syrian woman had forced me to concede that salvation wasn't restricted to Jews. But my encounter with her had taken place in a foreign land, and word hadn't filtered through to the area around the lake. On their home ground, I was loath to raise the subject in front of men whose outstanding devotion to the Law I respected in other ways.

We were now in Capernaum. Here, in the town where I was born, I would have to take a stand in front of the Pharisees who had educated me, as well as my former neighbours.

A major centre for collecting tolls, the town is home to a garrison of mostly non-Roman auxiliaries, whom the army employs to man outposts that are a long way from Rome, and who are less hostile towards Jews than the Romans themselves. Walking towards me I saw a centurion, accompanied by the usual group of Pharisees, among whom I recognized some of those I had clashed with from the start.

He came up to me respectfully, and begged me in slightly halting Greek:

"Sir, my *pais* is lying at home in terrible distress, and is going to die…"

He called me *kyrie*, or "sir" – so it was the man he was addressing, not the rabbi. And he used the word *pais*, which can mean "boy" as well as "servant". But what did that matter, it was obvious what he wanted: he was begging me to heal someone who was close to him. I was moved by his anguish, which was plain to see, but he was a Gentile, so I couldn't go to his house without making myself unclean. As with the Syrian woman, I reminded him of this:

"You want me to come and cure him?"

The centurion must have been stationed in the town for quite some time, because he seemed to know immediately why I had refused. I will never forget what he said, nor the way in which he said it.

"*Kyrie*, I am not worthy to have you come under my roof, but only speak the word and my *pais* will be healed!"

Once more the lava of the wilderness surged up within me; I was shaken to the depths of my being. Like all those who had overcome the obstacles of shame or social convention, he believed in the power of my God, he was calling on life itself. I was about to tell him that his dear one had already been healed when he went on:

"For I too am a man set under authority, with soldiers under me, and I say to one 'Go!' and he goes, and to another 'Come!' and he comes…"

I stood in the middle of the street, rooted to the spot with amazement in full view of the people who had gathered round. Did he appreciate the significance of what he was saying? He had told me that he knew exactly *who I was*: a man like him, under the authority of my creator, yet capable, as he was, of mediating between God's sovereign power and what duty required of me – which was to relieve human suffering. Could I cure people from a distance? Other healers had proved they could. But someone who had the insight to understand the precise nature of my relationship with God, which enabled me to heal people, no, I hadn't come across that, not since I was by the Jordan. So with all my heart I told him this, then turned to the Pharisees:

"Truly I say to you, many will come from east and west and will sit and feast with Abraham, Isaac and Jacob in the Kingdom of God! But you, you will be thrown into the outer darkness, where there will be weeping and gnashing of teeth!"

The centurion could go back to his house. The faith he had shown in coming to me was justified – his *pais* was already healed.

A form of public declaration, these events were soon being discussed all over the town, and word spread throughout Galilee that the rabbi had said that the Jews would not enter the Kingdom of God! Yet I had only spoken to a handful of Pharisees, some of whom had known me since the day I was born and dismissed every word of my teaching. They accused me of craving recognition, although I had never said (or even implied) that I saw myself as the host who was giving this banquet, nor even that I would eventually have a place of honour among the guests. What was more, despite the fact that they believed in the resurrection of the dead and included this in their teaching, they weren't prepared to accept that I should bewitch the ordinary people with colourful descriptions of what happened *afterwards*, something of which no one had – nor should have – any knowledge.

What made my crime worse was that I had publicly claimed as fact something I had learnt from the Samaritan woman at the well in the noonday heat. The Law of Moses was no longer my sole guiding principle; I no longer felt bound by the commandments but by Jacob and the Patriarchs, by the Judaism that existed before the revelation on Mount Sinai. Not only was this Kingdom of mine open to every race and creed, Jew and Gentile alike, it belonged to all time.

No longer was I simply a rabbi carving out his individual path in a country that was simply the way it was, the focus of other nations' hostility, protecting himself from them behind the wall of a Law that was interpreted literally. I wasn't even a prophet of doom of the John the Baptist variety – I was dismantling the Jewish identity; a heretic whose cause would soon be joined by every lunatic, hothead and revolutionary in the land.

From that moment on, my critics among the local Pharisees became my sworn enemies. It wouldn't be long before they told their influential colleagues in Jerusalem about me.

35

If they were going to tolerate the existence of someone whose prestige overshadowed their own, then these local potentates expected me to produce a sign from above, one of those dramatic theophanies that shine out like gold among the annals of the prophets. I treated their demand with the contempt it deserved. But what of my disciples? I could tell that they would also have liked to see proof that substantiated the claims I made.

Proof? It was right there before their eyes. Hadn't they seen all the sick people being healed? I said to them: "If it is by the finger of God that I heal, then this is *proof* that the Kingdom of God has come to you!"

But they had never really left John the Baptist and the banks of the Jordan behind, and expected the apocalypse to come in a pillar of fire at any moment. For them, the advent of the Kingdom of God would surely be the awe-inspiring event that is part of the Jewish mindset – a chariot of fire descending from heaven, radiant angels standing round the throne of God, a brand-new temple covered in glittering diamonds… But a mental case foaming at the mouth in a synagogue, a little boy having an epileptic fit, a foul-smelling leper, a paralysed man! All they could see were a few miracles that eased some of the world's suffering.

So I told them again: "The Kingdom of God is with you, it is among you now!" A world was about to end, and end at this very moment for those who purified their hearts. But as long as there were still men in the grip of Evil, this world and its sorrows would live on. Running out of arguments, I eventually said:

"Joyful are your eyes, for they see! Truly I say to you, many prophets and kings longed to see what you see, but did not see it."

But joyful they were not. It pained me to see how they were torn between their illusions and a reality that they were unable to grasp. After all, they had left their families and livelihoods to follow me, and had stayed with me throughout my vicissitudes. Other people wouldn't have done the same, and I was acutely aware of my responsibility to them. So one day, when I had gone off to be alone for a while as was my wont, I was surprised when they came and asked me, rather self-consciously:

"Teach us to pray, as John the Baptist taught his disciples!"

A great tide of love swept over me. They were admitting that they were incapable of drawing near to the mystery, and seemed to grasp where the source of my teaching and powers of healing lay! I tried to tell them about how I had found the God of loving kindness, how we had to become a little child in his eyes, but I was confronted with the conventions of an entire nation, for whom praying means reciting the fixed prayers. The Baptist must have produced such a prayer for his disciples to use, and they were asking me to do the same for them... ever since they were children they had been used to repeating the eighteen Ritual Blessings every day.

Anxious to fit in with daily life, the Pharisees have suggested that when people are travelling they should use an abbreviated version of the prayer, just seven blessings. Hadn't we been on the road permanently since we left the Jordan? So I would give them a short prayer, which wouldn't begin with the hallowed invocation, "Blessed art Thou, O Lord our God, King of the Universe"... Instead they would address God as *Abba*, which is rather like saying "Daddy":

"When you pray, say '*Abba*', so everyone will know who you are..."

They looked shocked: God was never referred to by this baby name in any of the liturgical prayers. He was called "Father", with the note of respectful distance that befitted the Divine Majesty. To speak to God as a child does to his human father was an act of familiarity quite unimaginable for any Jew!

I assured them that this was how I spoke to God, it was indicative of my relationship with him. Didn't they understand? If they followed my example they would. I told them to speak to *Abba*, to ask that his Kingdom should come, to them and to those around them, that his will should be done on earth as it was in heaven. I included a request that was suited to our nomadic life – that we shouldn't go without our daily bread. And another one, which summed up the law of the heart, its never-ending and boundless mutual forgiveness. And then finally, echoing the torment I had suffered in the wilderness, that *Abba* should spare them this ordeal and deliver them from Evil.

They were astonished: was that it? The Gentiles gave great speeches to their gods, while the Pharisees and other devout Jews would stand praying in the synagogue at great length – but we only get a few sentences? I pointed out that these pious individuals would make sure that they happened to be standing on the street corner when the shofar sounded, so everyone could see them praying. But they should do the opposite; like me they should go to a deserted place and pray to *Abba* in secret. These few phrases were enough – because *Abba* knew what they needed long before they told him.

Just a few phrases which would open their hearts. And then, silence.

At sunset I went up the mountain, but they didn't come with me. I had done everything that is expected of a prophet: I had summed up my life in a few words, offered it to them in a few brief sentences. What came afterwards was none of my concern. Sooner or later they would have to travel the same road as me.

Tonight they lie scattered under the olive trees, fast asleep, while I stand here alone under the stars, face to face with you, *Abba*.

36

I was exhausted. These endless disputes! Yet they were part of the life of a Pharisee, his driving force, the breath of life. Hillel and Shammai had spent their lives pitted against each other and sometimes the people who came to listen to them, but they had never been confronted with a wall of silence like this: people might have disagreed with their opinions, but never had they refused to talk to them, rejected them outright. Nor had they had to watch as their words sank for ever into the quicksand of their disciples' minds.

With autumn came the Feast of Tabernacles, a family festival that commemorates the Exodus, and which Jews set great store by. After six months' absence it was an opportunity to return to Jerusalem, to submerge myself in the jubilant crowds as well as to see my family again. We would be passing through Capernaum, and I was hoping to make the trip with my four brothers as we had done in the past.

But they had changed. Loyal members of the local synagogue, they were as hostile towards me as the Pharisees.

"Leave here and go to Judaea," they said. "Let your disciples there also see the works you are doing; for no one who wants to be widely known acts in secret! If that is what you want, show yourself to the world."

It was only jealousy, lack of understanding – but I had learnt to hold my tongue. They would set off for the festival without me, taking the Twelve with them. I would stay behind in Galilee without family or disciples, as alone as I am here tonight.

Yet there was something in me that rebelled. None of the prophets had ever hidden when it came to proclaiming the coming of a new world of which he was the gatekeeper. This Kingdom wasn't mine, it was bursting forth while I looked on, the lava of the wilderness would sweep through the old Israel, put it to the flame. After hesitating for a few days I changed my mind and decided to go alone and in secret, just one more nameless pilgrim in the crowd.

I would go to Jerusalem. Whatever the cost.

The courtyards and balconies of the city were decked with branches, symbolizing the tents in which the Israelites had lived in the wilderness during the first Exile. Excited children were building shelters in the street, which brought smiles to the faces of the old and made mothers dewy-eyed.

In the midst of the joyful throng I came across the Judaean. He was even more worried than on my last visit: there were members of the Sanhedrin who weren't prepared to tolerate my antics any longer, and were wondering how to silence this bumptious little rabbi. Caiaphas, the High Priest, had listened to them but was playing for time. He reminded them that no Jew can be found guilty unless he has committed a crime; our respect for the Law is what sets us apart from the Gentiles. But if I appeared in public during the festival, they would have to put me to the test.

The Judaean wanted to know if I was going to stay out of sight at Lazarus's house like last time?

I told him about recent events, my encounter with the Syrian woman and the centurion in Capernaum. How during the course of my constant journeying my teaching had gradually developed, giving my healings their true meaning; how I had left the pessimism of John the Baptist behind and created a time and a place by proclaiming a Kingdom that was to come, yet which had already arrived.

This was what I wanted now: I had to teach in the Temple, the sounding board of Israel.

He was silent for quite a while before replying, a habit I much valued. A fellow disciple of the Baptist, he was able to appreciate how far I had come, and would be with me every morning on the esplanade of Solomon, where the crowds come to listen to preachers of all persuasions. In the evening, however, he would leave me in the Garden of Gethsemane, where I would find the solitude that he knew was vital to me.

I accepted both proposals: he would accompany me during the day, and I would withdraw into seclusion at night. It was comforting to have an understanding friend in this time of twilight, whose end neither of us was yet able to see.

My appearance on the esplanade shortly after daybreak the next morning didn't go unnoticed. The number of passers-by who thronged to listen to me was an indication of the extent to which my fame had spread beyond Galilee. There were Jews from Judaea and Transjordan, Hellenized Jews from Egypt or Syria... all peddling terrifying predictions about the end of the world that lent weight to the texts that were doing the rounds, apocalyptic visions attributed to Daniel or Baruch, manuscripts copied out by the Essenes. They were eager to hear what he had to say, this rabbi from Galilee who described the hereafter as a banquet and told people how to get themselves on the guest list.

I sat at the base of a pillar, sheltered from the September sunlight that was already warming the venerable marble paving. The small crowd who pressed around me restricted my view of the vast esplanade, from where we could just hear a vague murmur.

All of a sudden, drifting over people's heads came other, barely audible sounds, followed by shouts of "Death! Death!" A ripple ran through the crowd; I asked the Judaean what was happening. He said the Sanhedrin had recently heard the case of a woman who had been caught with a man who wasn't her husband. According to the Law, by committing adultery she rendered herself gravely impure, something that could only be absolved by her public execution within the Temple precinct.

The Roman occupier reserves the right to hear cases of a political nature and impose a sentence of death by crucifixion. But in this vast Empire made up of a patchwork of different nationalities and creeds, Rome delegates responsibility for judging religious matters to the relevant local authorities. Under Jewish Law, adultery is punished by public stoning: so this woman would die under a hail of stones while her lover, protected by his status as a man, was spared.

I stayed where I was. Jostling through the crowd, a group of Pharisees came towards me, followed by a group of men in a state of great agitation, all carrying stones. With them they were dragging a woman, whom they threw at my feet, at the same time pulling off her veil, and then stood looking me up and down with mocking expressions. The eldest of the Pharisees spoke up, as much for the benefit of the crowd as for mine:

"Rabbi, this woman was caught in the very act of committing adultery. In the Law Moses commands us to stone such women. Now what do you say?"

Everyone went quiet. This controversial rabbi was going to have to take sides, we weren't by the lake now, this was the nerve centre of God's Chosen People. Among them I recognized one or two of the Pharisees who had come to investigate me in Galilee. This was too good an opportunity to miss, they were going to seize it with both hands, push me into a corner.

So what was it to be – the unflinching enforcement of the Law of Moses, yes or no? Put the woman to death in front of me with my approval… or would I rebel against the natural order of things as decreed by Moses himself?

I looked down and closed my eyes. What crime had this woman committed, except that of loving? Once again I saw the prostitute at Simon the Pharisee's house, felt her tears falling on my feet. Knowing she was forgiven had restored her to herself, she had been reborn before my very eyes. Even when it is blameworthy, can love really be a crime? And who are we to impose conditions on it?

Not visible to my lowered gaze, the Pharisees were telling me in loud voices that they wouldn't allow me to shy away from my obligations yet again. I glanced up at the woman, then bent down and wrote in the dust on the paving stones with my finger. The first stone wouldn't strike her square on the forehead, it would take several blows before she staggered and fell. Then someone would go over with a large cobblestone and splatter her brains across the marble paving of the Temple. And the men would feel satisfied.

I sat up, gestured to the woman to stand up in the midst of them, then looked these pillars of society in the eye.

"Let anyone among you who is without sin be the first to throw a stone at her."

And I bent down and started writing in the dust again, so as not to have to reply. I wasn't going to argue with them or plead for mercy. It is true that our Law is quite clear on this point, the woman's actions warranted the death penalty, but we had to go back to the beginning, before Moses was given the Law on Mount Sinai, to the moment when the world was created.

While God rested from his labours on the seventh day, wasn't the Evil One still hard at work inside each of us? Couldn't I myself feel his teeth in me every minute of the day? Could he be killed by throwing stones at him? When the king invites guests to a marriage feast, does he stone them to death? He doesn't drive anyone away, he opens his doors to everyone, even passers-by. The Kingdom isn't a courtroom, the banquet takes precedence over the Law. This woman shouldn't be buried under a pile of stones, but reborn. From this moment on she was one of the guests.

Not hearing a sound, I looked up. One by one and silently the Pharisees walked away, led by the Elder of the Sanhedrin. Arms hanging limply by their sides, trying not to be noticed, most of the men placed the stones back on the ground. The crowd was struck dumb, like an amphitheatre full of people turned to stone around a statue in their midst.

"Woman, where are they? Has no one condemned you?"

For the first time her face came alive.

"No one, Rabbi."

I leant against the pillar, feeling a sudden pain in my back.

"Neither do I condemn you. Go your way, and from now on do not sin again."

Once more a ripple ran through the crowd. And I saw men picking up stones to throw at me.

37

The Judaean led me through the streets and alleyways, forcing
his way through the crowds. When the first stones began flying
in my direction, he dragged me behind the pillar, then out of the
large double doors that leads from the Temple precinct into the
Old Town, which he knew inside out. As we went, at something
between a walk and a run, we discussed what had happened. I had
taken the woman's side, yes, but defending someone accused of a
crime doesn't mean that you should share their fate. So why did
the men of Israel want to stone me? He replied that firstly it was
because I had publicly reminded the notables from the Sanhedrin
that they were sinners like everyone else, and that God alone has
the power of life and death. But most of all, by telling the woman
that I didn't condemn her I had counted myself among sinners
like themselves; at that point I had forfeited my status as God's
messenger, and ceased to be the heaven-sent hero that the crowds
were expecting. Being familiar with the way their minds worked,
my friend thought they were throwing stones at an icon that had
brought destruction upon itself.

He may have been right, but all I had seen was the woman staring
at me. The sight of it struck me with the force of lightning flashing
across the night sky; I can still see her unequivocal, smouldering

gaze: I hadn't only saved her from a terrible death, I had opened the gates of the Kingdom for her. She knew this, had told me as much without saying a word in the fleeting moment before she vanished into the crowd who were baying for my blood.

Here, tonight, that is why I am no longer afraid. The gaze of two different women has made me bold, and they will remain with me till the end.

We made our way to the south gate, where we were met by my disciples. They had witnessed the events on the esplanade from a distance, horrified at the sight of the worthies from the Sanhedrin and the hate-filled crowd. My unexpected stance had unleashed a storm of questions in their minds, for which they had no answers. If we are all sinners, they said, including the highest authorities in Israel and you yourself, then where does Evil come from? Who can be held to account for their actions if everything we do is foreordained? Are we riven by sin from the moment we are born, or...

They went up to a beggar who had been blind from birth, and used him as an example:

"And him, Rabbi? Who sinned, this man or his parents, that he was born blind?"

"Neither this man nor his parents!"

I walked over to the blind man, spat on the ground, made mud with my saliva and spread it over his unseeing eyes. Then I told him to go and wash in the nearby pool of Siloam. Mud is no different from the dust that God used to create the first man. If the blind man regained his sight, might my disciples then understand?

When he came back he couldn't believe his eyes, which could now see for the very first time. The whole district was soon buzzing with the news, and the people who lived nearby began saying to each other excitedly:

"It is him!" said some of them. "No, it is someone like him!" said others.

With a smile he told them: "It really is me!"

"So... how were your eyes opened?"

However many times they asked, he never tired of telling them about the man called Jesus, the mud he spread on his eyes, the pool – and that was all it took, he could see. Then they asked: "So where is he, this Jesus?" He had no idea, because at that point he was still blind, so he could only hear his voice. But he had had faith in him and did what he told him to do.

This marvel in human form was a matter for the authorities. He was taken by the hand and dragged to the nearest synagogue. The Judaean advised me to leave the area quietly, there was a danger I might be recognized, and then I would have the Pharisees to deal with all over again. He would go after the crowd and report back to me later.

The very next day he came to Lazarus's house in Bethany, where I had sought sanctuary. With a smile he told me how events had turned out. The former blind man had been taken to the local Pharisees, but once they had got him to tell them what had happened they didn't believe him. So they summoned his parents:

"Is this your son, who you say was born blind? How then does he now see?"

Terrified and fearing the worst for their son and themselves, they answered:

"We know that this is our son, and that he was born blind. But we do not know how it is that he now sees, or who opened his eyes. We don't know; ask him, he is of age. He will speak for himself and tell you what happened."

So they called the man in for a second time, and asked him to tell them everything again, from the beginning. Losing patience, and with the crowd on his side, he got angry and stormed out of the synagogue, slamming the door behind him under a hail of insults from the Pharisees. The story was soon all over the city, embellished by each new telling.

After the paralysed man at Beth-zatha this was the second healing I had performed in Jerusalem, and on both occasions I was met with a hostile reaction from the authorities. The Judaean suggested that I leave the city and not come back until next Passover – in six months everything would be forgotten.

So once again I was forced to run away. I decided to leave the next day and return to the Jordan, where everything began when I met John the Baptist. I would go back to my origins, to people for whom he was still very much alive, and where they might listen to me more than they did here, in this city blinded by power and fanatical belief.

38

Until Passover of the following year we spent our time roaming around the course of the Jordan, usually on the right bank, although occasionally crossing into Gentile territory on the other side. Through my healings, the Beatitudes, the law of the heart and proclaiming the Kingdom, I had taken on the mantle of Elijah. I have always refused to put forward my teaching as a formal system; until the very end I preferred to be guided by the reactions of the people who came to listen to me – although the more I whittled away at the foundations of Jewish society, the more hostile these became.

In the first place, our nomadic life offended pious Jews who set great store by traditional family structures. Not only had my disciples left hearth and home to follow me, but wives would occasionally abandon their husbands so they could travel with us for a while. Every month these women were tainted by bleeding, as well as being obliged to visit the graves of relatives – so how, when and where could they perform the appointed and highly personal purification rites? No one dared question me on the subject, but the fact that my teaching never alluded to matters of legal impurity spoke volumes.

But those in high places weren't satisfied with my tacit silence. In due course a delegation of Pharisees arrived to question me:

"In your opinion, is it lawful for a man to put away his wife?"

They had clearly been sent from Jerusalem, where the authorities now wished to put their suspicions about me on a legal footing.

Throughout the Empire, even beyond its borders, divorce is standard practice. Jewish Law doesn't express an opinion on this, it simply codifies it. A man can put away his wife and marry another for any reason whatsoever; his rejected wife then has to remarry so as not to be without the protection of a man. But if her second husband dies or she is divorced for a second time, she isn't allowed to go back to her first husband, since for him (and him alone) she is now ritually impure. This point of law was unpalatable to the wider population, who took a dim view of such spurned women who were unable to marry for a third time, and who in order to live were forced into a life of prostitution – a grave state of impurity.

I replied with a question:

"What did Moses command?"

"Moses allowed a man to write a certificate of dismissal and to put away his wife."

By endorsing this law in their presence I would be publicly supporting the threat of abjection that hangs over every abandoned wife and thus siding with the establishment against popular sentiment. It would also be as good as admitting that the women who accompanied me ran the same risks as wives who have been rejected; by travelling with us, far away from their husbands, were they too not deprived of a natural protector? By allowing them near me, wouldn't people say that I was encouraging them to prostitute themselves – possibly with me? Once again it warranted stoning.

I was caught in their trap.

Out of respect for the Sabbath and the tradition of oaths, as on previous occasions I had to answer with circumspection. No, I wasn't rejecting the Law of Moses outright, I was calling

THE SILENCE OF GETHSEMANE

on a higher one, which had been engraved in man's heart from the moment God created him. It was no longer enough simply to interpret the Law, the Pharisees had to undergo a change of heart. I told them this quite plainly, then settled the matter in my usual way:

"From the beginning of creation, God made them male and female. For this reason a man shall leave his father and mother and be joined to his wife, and the two shall become one flesh. So whoever puts away his wife and marries another commits adultery!"

For the second time I had declared one of the laws of Moses void. Even worse, I was decreeing that any Jew who obeyed this law to the letter and divorced his wife in order to marry another was committing adultery. So in the presence of witnesses, I had said that following the Law could be sinful. But resorting to the story of the Creation as a means of revoking part of the legislative code wasn't allowed: no one can use the Law against the Law. From being just a controversial rabbi, I had become a blasphemer.

Jerusalem would draw its own conclusions from that.

However, I had also hurt the feelings of the devout Jews in the audience. In our society, people rarely marry for love, it is chiefly a way of bearing children for the People of the Covenant. But I was claiming that if God created man and woman, it was in order to be joined in the flesh. By this I implied that his primary intention for marriage was pleasure – shared pleasure – and not procreation. My listeners were deeply unsettled by this allusion to sexual gratification, which was usually provided for them by the prostitutes who could be found anywhere.

We meddle with sexual taboos and the deep-seated instincts they conceal at our peril. My popularity with the conservative wing of the audience began to falter. How far away it was now, that Galilean springtime!

Deep down, the Jews have always pined for the time of the Patriarchs, when the One God was a palpable presence amid the bar-
renness of the wilderness, before a wall of commandments was
erected between him and them.

That era seemed to be long gone. Left destitute and divided by
Roman rule, my fellow countrymen's overriding concern was now
simply to survive, they were desperate for certainties, irrefutable
facts – whereas I was following the intuition that came to me in the
wilderness, that of an experience which was beyond words. They
were captivated by what I said, but it only raised questions when
what they needed was answers.

For me, the Beatitudes, the law of the heart and the coming
Kingdom were all connected by a single, unifying theme, that of a
return to the moment of creation. Did this mean a new beginning
of the world, another Genesis? For those who came to listen to
me this was no substitute for an organized, well-structured plan
of campaign that everyone could understand.

Increasingly I appeared to be on the fringe of a nation that
was on the wane in this second decade of the century. Prompted
by Israel's evident state of decline, some people have chosen
to cut themselves off from society, but I was no Essene, nor
was I a Zealot, and I had distanced myself from my former
Baptist friends. There was little doubt that I would be found
guilty by the authorities in Jerusalem, and I ate quite openly
at the houses of profiteers, associated with sinners and spoke
to strange women, made no secret of my admiration for a
centurion from the occupying forces. I had healed Gentile as
well as Jewish children. I had replaced the purity laws with
an ill-defined law of inner purity; in other words, for the traditional code of actions I had substituted one of intent. But
who was able to tell what someone's intentions were? How
could they be assessed?

In a word, I was an unknown quantity. I no longer spoke the same language as the ordinary Jewish people. And, this country being what it is, there is no place for a Jew who doesn't fit into a category.

Like the more conservative members of my audience, the Twelve now realized this. Although I wasn't aware of it at the time, this starry night in the silence of Gethsemane was already close at hand.

39

The question of boundaries was one that refused to go away. God had made a covenant with the Jews, and with them alone – so on the Last Day, what would become of the Gentiles? Shocked by what I had said to the Roman centurion, the senior Pharisees weren't content to let matters rest. Several of their jurists, who didn't wish to sever connections completely, came to see me on a number of occasions for a private, friendly discussion.

One day a Scribe came down from Jerusalem, seeking to put the question in legal terms: was the Law of Moses universal, or did it only apply to God's Chosen People?

I quoted the golden rule of the Greeks: "Do as you would be done by." Although this was known the world over, I told him that I preferred the Jewish version, as used by Rabbi Hillel: "That which you do not wish others to do to you, do not to your neighbour: this is all of the Law, the rest is just commentary." I added that I liked to express it in more positive terms: "That which you would like others to do to you, do the same to them: this is the Law and the teaching of the prophets."

"So in the Law," he answered, "which commandment is the first of all?"

A small crowd had gathered and was listening closely to our discussion. The Scribe appeared to be unusually receptive towards me, but he didn't want to leave without hearing my reply. For isn't putting the commandments in order of priority the chief activity of every learned Jew?

So I said: "The first is…" and then, closing my eyes, I chanted the *Shema Yisrael*, the verse from the Law with which every prayer in the synagogue begins:

"…the first is, 'Hear, O Israel: the Lord our God, the Lord is one; you shall love the Lord your God with all your heart, and with all your soul, and with all your mind, and with all your strength.'"

On hearing the familiar chant, the Scribe and all the people immediately joined in, swaying back and forth. Anyone who hasn't seen Jews praying spontaneously in the street will never understand the Jewish soul, and where this ravaged and divided nation gets its remarkable strength.

I went on:

"And the second is similar: 'You shall love your neighbour as yourself.' There is no other commandment greater than these."

I could see that the Scribe was surprised, but he soon collected himself:

"You are right, Rabbi! You have truly said that he is One, and besides him there is no other, and to love him with all the heart, and with all the understanding, and with all the strength, and to love one's neighbour as oneself, this is much more important than all the burnt offerings and sacrifices in the Temple!"

It was my turn to be surprised. There was nothing unusual about a Pharisee maligning the Sadducees, who as a caste make a handsome living out of the Temple and its trade in animals. But for one of the intellectuals among them to agree that love should come before the study of and obedience to the commandments was unexpected. I replied:

"You are not far from the Kingdom of God…"

My words were almost drowned out by the muttering of the crowd that had gathered. Love of God and love of one's neighbour are two quite separate commandments that are never combined into a single rule of life. Our rabbis always refer to and comment on them individually, but to my audience, amalgamating them into one commandment that was greater than all the rest was unheard of as well as scandalous.

Sensing their discomfiture, the Scribe returned to the attack:

"So… who is my neighbour?"

Hadn't he heard about what I had said to the centurion in Capernaum? As there were so many people present, I decided to express it differently this time, using a parable. I told the story of the man who was set upon by Zealots along the way, who left him for dead at the roadside. First a priest, and then a Jew who was an acolyte in the Temple passed by on the other side without stopping. Then a Samaritan – a foreign heretic – came along, saw the man lying on the ground, took pity on him, helped him to his feet, tended to his wounds and took him to an inn, where he paid his board and lodging for as long as it would take him to recover. So which of these three was a neighbour to the injured man?

"The one who showed him mercy," answered the Scribe.

"Go and do likewise!"

After he had left I wondered if I had won him over. And had I won over the crowd? They just stood there around me, not moving, not saying a word. Among the many eyes I sought out those of my disciples – but they were nowhere to be seen.

Until now they had always been with me whenever I was teaching, pondering on what I said for a long time afterwards. So had they found something better to do with their time? Had they lost interest in the issue of boundaries, something that has preyed on Jewish minds since the world began?

Or... were they now drifting away from a rabbi who hadn't lived up to their expectations?

Because my definition of what constitutes a "neighbour" must have left them deeply troubled. For a Jew, a neighbour can only be a fellow Jew – never a Gentile. For the Essenes, a neighbour is someone who belongs to their sect – never another Jew. To the Zealots, a neighbour is someone who is involved in the same political struggle as they are. And even if some of my disciples had spent time with the Essenes, and others with the Zealots, they still had the archetypal characteristics of ordinary Jews, who set store by the traditional, hierarchical world of the precepts.

Nonetheless, I had been careful to rank these two love commandments in first and second place. Love of God wasn't diminished by association with love of our neighbour; love of our neighbour always has its origins in God. I was simply saying that we can't know or love God (who is invisible to our eyes) if we disregard or spurn our neighbour – a neighbour who isn't a brother in arms or a member of the same religion, race or political party, but just a man, woman or child whom we happen to meet along the way.

This new thinking flew in the face of everything they had been taught. Our rabbis don't turn love into a law: love doesn't issue commands, it exists by scrupulously obeying the rules. You would no more comment on it than you would on the air you breathe.

I wanted our neighbour to become the oxygen that breathes life into love.

I realized that with this I was putting the finishing touches to my teaching, and that I had helped bring out the best in Judaism. Yet when it came to those around me, it seemed to fall on deaf ears. I saw the Twelve rebuffing children whose mothers innocently brought them to the rabbis so they could give them their blessing – was it fitting for the future King of Israel to stoop to such childish behaviour, which was unworthy of him and his aides? They brushed them aside with a wave of the hand, which made me angry:

"Let the little children come to me; do not stop them! For it is to such as these that the Kingdom of God belongs!"

Children! They are the ones who run around gaily and unconstrainedly in village halls where feasts are held, climbing onto the host's lap and cuddling up to him without a second thought! They are the living image of my Kingdom. But for my disciples as much as for my audience, it was a mirage on a distant horizon, and they showed no sign of wanting to set off along the road that led to it.

So I was left alone to stare at the stars and dream.

Then suddenly reality burst in, when some Pharisee friends came to warn me:

"Get away from here, for Herod wants to kill you!"

I would later discover that Herod – a slave to superstition and wracked with remorse for having had John the Baptist beheaded – believed I was the reincarnation of the prophet of the Jordan. He wanted to summon me before him so he could question me. The moment I was in his clutches it would be easy for the Sanhedrin to have me moved from Galilee to Jerusalem, where by now there was enough evidence against me for them to put me on trial. There was little doubt what the outcome would be.

I had to escape, get across the border.

The Evil One had gained the upper hand; from now on my life was in danger.

Part III

Born to Be Killed

The flimsy but unyielding strands of the demon's web.

Rimbaud

40

Ever since the first day of creation, Evil has acted on the world stage.

There isn't a single deserted spot, not a blasted heath or corner of a crowded town or city where he doesn't perform. Here he takes a pace back, there he skirts round an obstacle, attacks from the flank, from behind, from every direction. Down through the ages his victories have come in swift succession, he finds his way into the slightest crack, burrows and tears away at it until he makes it bigger, deeper. He weaves himself into the fabric of everyday life, creates its desires, its anxieties, its every act of brutality. He divides, destroys and demolishes, thriving on the chaos he has caused.

Then he dances for joy in the ruins.

Having tried to eliminate me when I was first in the wilderness, he revealed himself openly in the synagogue in Capernaum. In a sense, it was at that moment that we recognized each other. Ever since then I had come up against him constantly in people who were mentally ill, in the bedridden, the blind, those who were close to death, even in words that came from Peter's mouth. It was an exhausting hand-to-hand combat.

I thought I would win victories. Dredge the stream of prophecy that runs beside the great river of the Law, make the human heart its source; reveal who our neighbour is, that woman isn't created to be ruled by man but to unite with him in carnal bliss; make happiness – not hellfire – the stuff out of which this new creation is woven; address God as *Abba*, replace fear with loving kindness.

Reunify. Bring enemies together, unite neighbour with neighbour, man with woman, and each and every one of us with the Invisible. But the relentless dance of Evil shattered my dreams of unity. In the fight against Evil I would now be confronted with people in powerful positions; there was a chance I might be silenced, like John the Baptist. I think we were still on the Syrian border when I decided to tell my disciples one last parable, which would sum up everything that I had tried to explain to them about the Kingdom and about themselves, as well as about God.

I asked them to gather round, as I had on that warm, sunny day beside a field in Galilee when everything still seemed possible, when I had spoken of sowing and reaping. They sat round me in a circle in the gathering dusk, along with one or two others. How far away it was, the time of multitudes beside the lake! And I began by saying:

"There was a man who had two sons…"

The man was wealthy. One day, out of the blue, the younger of his sons asked for his share of the property that he would one day inherit. Saddened, the father couldn't refuse, and his son left the family home. He wanted to travel to distant lands, experience life, but he would squander his money on extravagant living… And his father guessed right. Because after a while, the young man found that both his pockets and his belly were empty. In order to survive he hired himself out to a farmer, looking after pigs.

The power of parables! In the lengthening shadows I could see the faces of the people around me beginning to fall as I described the son's sorry state, how he would have been happy to eat the swill that he poured into the troughs, how he missed his father's house where the hired hands were treated better than he was now. In the depths of despair he decided to go home and face his father's anger. What would he say in his defence? He would admit his guilt. He would accept the punishment he was given, he deserved it, it was only right. And he worked out what he would say, learnt it off by heart:

"Father, I have sinned against heaven and before you; I am no longer worthy to be called your son. Treat me like one of your hired hands."

From the look in the Twelve's eyes I could tell that they were picturing the scene, the young fellow in rags, trudging barefoot along the road, repeating his plea over and over so he didn't forget it... He was going to be put through the mill, that was for sure, humiliated, rebuked by his father – and rightly so! They were waiting to hear what would happen next, hanging on my every word like in the early days in Galilee.

But during all the time he had been away, the father, who was consumed with worry, had never stopped looking out for him. His heart was bleeding, he wanted only one thing in the whole world, for his son to come back. Then one day, in the shimmering heat in the distance he saw a figure that looked like one of the many vagrants who passed by that way, and immediately knew it was him.

"He was filled with compassion, and ran and put his arms around him and kissed him!"

Surprised by the unexpected ending, my disciples were wondering what the wretched young man would say. He would hang his head in shame and begin the little speech that he had memorized:

"Father, I have sinned against heaven and before you; I am no longer worthy to be called your son..."

But his father stopped him, put his hand over his mouth so he couldn't finish what he was saying: Not one more word, he said, I know, I imagined it all, the hardships, the suffering, the shame. Eyes welling with tears of joy, he turned to his servants, who had come to revel in the young master's sorry state, watch him being punished.

"Quickly!" he said. "Bring out a robe – the best one – and put it on him! And then get me a ring to put on his finger, and... sandals for his feet! And then..."

And then they had to go to the herd and pick out the fattest calf, and kill it, and then prepare...

"And then let us eat and celebrate! For this son of mine was dead and is alive again; he was lost and is found!"

In the dark of evening I could see the Twelve's eyes shining brightly. There was no such thing as a dead end, there was always the joy of being reborn into God's loving kindness, a feast that lasted for all eternity! As I was speaking I was filled with the same compassion as the father, felt my eyes filling with his tears.

When I had finished, I realized I would never be able to tell them any more than this. If they hadn't understood tonight, then perhaps after I was dead they might remember this parable.

Because of Herod's police, when we got back to the lake we kept ourselves to ourselves. Some of my Pharisee friends came to see me. I was wise to keep out of sight; in Jerusalem, my defence of the woman who had committed adultery had been rejected, it was possible that the Pharisees and the Sadducees would join forces against me. Here, on the other hand, I was perfectly safe, people in Galilee were as quick to forget as they were to flare up. The crowds had stopped coming to listen to me, so if I kept quiet I would have nothing to fear.

Should I heed their advice? Is a prophet born to stay in hiding, smother the flames of his teaching for fear they might burn him? If I refused to concede defeat, then I alone would suffer the consequences. I didn't have children to watch grow up, no wife to look after, no mother to cosset, no brothers any more; no friends around me, just supporters and opponents.

Perhaps not even any disciples.

On another occasion I had just been telling them about the very real danger I was in, hoping to get a few crumbs of comfort, perhaps some fellow feeling from them. I think we were either at Zebedee's house or somewhere nearby, when I saw his two sons, James and John, the Boanerges, coming towards me. In full view of everyone they took me to one side.

"Rabbi," they said, loudly enough for the others to hear, "we want you to do for us whatever we ask of you."

"*You want!*... And what is it you want me to do for you?"

"Grant us to sit, one at your right hand and one at your left, in your glory."

Poor souls! They were still drifting around in the murky back-waters of their imaginings. They had no idea what they were asking. If the future held anything for me, it was less likely to be power and glory than it was a very bitter cup: were they able to drink it too? Certainly, they replied, with staggering self-confidence that only went to show how out of touch they were with reality – and with their rabbi. But the other ten came and put a stop to our private conversation: they had heard everything, and they weren't about to let this conniving pair manipulate their way into the two senior positions without doing something about it!

Taken aback, I walked away and left them to shout and argue. Zebedee's wife immediately seized her chance, taking her sons' place and begging me on bended knees to help secure their advancement. So behind each of my disciples loomed an ex-tended family whose members had only one thing in mind – to use me to procure preferential treatment for them, create a brighter future.

No longer were the Twelve content to imagine what it would be like to occupy the best positions, they were fighting among themselves to get their hands on them.

I glanced at Judas. Iscariot didn't say a word, he wasn't going to get involved with their dispute.

41

In this wake-like atmosphere there were still one or two dignitaries who came to see me, almost covertly. Such as the Scribe from Galilee who claimed that he would follow me wherever I went. I replied that foxes have holes and the birds of the air have nests, but that I didn't even have a stone on which to lay my head. He nodded in dignified fashion, and I never saw him again.

Another episode springs to mind, one that is indicative of the sense of abandonment and euphoria with which Jews are simultaneously afflicted. Seeing me walking past, an elegantly dressed young man rushed over and prostrated himself in front of me. I helped him up and asked what he wanted. From his candid manner I could tell straight away that he was from a good family, had had an excellent education and would inherit a fortune.

"Good Rabbi, what must I do to inherit eternal life?"

At the very first word my hackles rose. *Good* was one of the ways in which cultured Jews refer to God so as not to use his name. He received a terse reply:

"Why do you call me 'Good'? No one is Good but God alone!"

There were any number of people like this in Israel, confused, noble-minded and gullible, quick to idolize the first passer-by who was able to catch their attention and entice them away to some Eldorado. *Never* would I be a god, not for him or for anyone else. Before even answering his question I wanted him to understand this, even if it meant hurting his feelings. But seeing his confusion I controlled myself; after all he was only a child, he couldn't help being naive:

"You know the commandments..."

And I listed some of the precepts of the Law, particularly the honour that he owed his parents. For him, no one could take their place in his heart.

"Rabbi," he answered, "I have kept all these since my childhood."

I looked into his eyes. They were so unclouded, as clear and fresh as a mountain stream! If I had had a son I would have liked him to be like this; a son who, like me, would give up the comforts of home to follow in my footsteps, carry on with and complete what I had set out to do... Almost fondly, I told him something that was quite unthinkable: that he had been given everything in life, and had done all that Judaism asks of the Righteous. To be able to go into the feast, he lacked only one thing, that utter receptivity which is found in children:

"Go, sell what you own, and give the money to the poor; then come, follow me!"

Anxiously I waited for him to reply. Was he prepared to go that far?

His eyes clouded over, his face lost its serene expression. Then slowly he turned and walked away, eyes downcast.

Now I have nothing more to look forward to in life, the thought of the young man who aroused the very feelings of affection that I had chosen to put behind me, the image of him bowed beneath the burden of his wealth weighs heavily on me, like remorse that is too great to bear. So was it impossible for some people to enter the Kingdom, as difficult as it is to thread a needle?

I have to believe that for God nothing is impossible.

Tonight, I *owe it* to myself to believe it.

These painful memories have shaken me out of the listlessness that was gradually taking hold of me in the cool night air. I am not in Galilee now, but in the olive grove, looking across at the walls of Jerusalem and the Temple in the light of a full, Passover moon. How long have I been here, keeping watch? On the other side of the Kidron Valley, the sound of the crowds seems to be fading into the darkness, it must be late by now.

Why hasn't the Judaean come to find us? What unforeseen event has upset the insane plans that he was telling me about earlier this evening? It's as clear as daylight now. I duck under the branches and go over to my disciples. They're still asleep in the clearing, lying at the base of the trees like dead leaves. I'm not going to wake them. If it is to be tonight, then there is nothing more that they or I can do. All we can do is wait.

I've come back to the friendly tree, to lean against it. There is still time for me to be alone with my thoughts, with the dark of the night.

42

During this dormant period far away from Jerusalem I had time to withdraw into myself, to reflect on Hillel's enigmatic words: "If we are not here, who is here? And if we are here, who is here?"

It is only now that I am able to understand what he meant. Who is God? Who is He? A Jew never asks this question, He is just *here*. The proof of God's existence lies in creation itself, the heavens that tell of His glory. Yet this is also evidence that the Jew himself exists, that he stands before the star-studded firmament.

When I was in the wilderness, this fact had struck me very forcefully: if I wasn't here, face to face with myself as well as with Him, then God didn't exist. Later I became aware of the new relationship that had grown up between Him and me.

If I am *here*, then it is He that is within me, father and mother at once. The Kingdom is a constant interaction with a familiar God – an impulse that was followed by all the prophets.

For the Pharisees, however, God has come to live on earth in a house, the Temple in Jerusalem. His ineffable Glory – the *Shekhinah* – dwells there physically, in a hidden cavity in the Holy of Holies. It is the only place where it is possible for the divine and the human to meet. In our language we use the word *moed*, which means both *meeting* and *feast*. When I told people that they must

be aware who their neighbour was, I was giving them a foretaste
of this feast, and thus fulfilling the word of the Jewish prophets.

Now that my disciples had lost interest, and I found myself in
conflict with the authorities as well as abandoned by the crowds in
Galilee, this feast was something I could experience only inwardly,
in the silent chamber of my heart. It was almost Passover, the third
since I left the Jordan. Regardless of the risks, it was in the Temple
that I had to celebrate something that for me was now little more
than the ghost of a festival.

It was then I received word that Lazarus was ill; his sisters were
asking me to come to him in the house in Bethany that was now a
second home for me. But I hesitated: I still had the respect of a few
Pharisees here in Galilee, there was my family, and if the crowds
no longer flocked to hear me as they once had, they hadn't actually turned against me. Whereas by going to Jerusalem I would
be walking straight into what John the Baptist called the fiery
furnace. So should I declare the contest open, put my head into
the lion's mouth?

For two whole days I didn't do anything, as if powerless to make
a decision. If Mary and Martha had sent for me, it was because
Lazarus was dying. Yet I sensed that my own journey was coming
to an end as well. Pursued by Herod, disowned by the Sanhedrin,
if I did go, the only way to save my life would be to yield to them
publicly. But had any of the prophets of Israel ever yielded?

After two days, the decision took itself. I called my disciples
and told them:

"We are going back to Judaea."

"Rabbi," they objected, "the Jews were just now trying to stone
you, and are you going there again?"

They were right. The stones that had been piled up ready for
the adulteress would still be there, beside the Temple esplanade.

Jerusalem, Jerusalem, the city that kills prophets and stones those who are sent to it! We were on a hillside overlooking the lake. I took one last look at the gently rolling landscape, the fishermen's houses with their roofs made of branches, the little boats drawn up on the shore. I saw myself as a child, running through the narrow streets and alleyways of Capernaum, evenings spent in the warm, damp air that rose from the still water, my mother crouched over the fireplace whose flames cast red shadows over her face... But I hadn't come into the world to live a life of tranquillity.

No one is a prophet in his own lifetime. As Elijah's successor, I was born to be killed. And what better place for a prophet to die than in Jerusalem?

Without another word to my disciples, I set my face to go south.

43

As we made our way along by the Jordan I went on ahead by myself, separated from the Twelve, who followed behind, sweating with fright. We had to move aside to let dispatch riders gallop past; the Roman garrison in Caesarea was being sent to reinforce Jerusalem. The same as every year, thousands of pilgrims were expected for the Passover. Several times in the past, this great gathering of Jews from every corner of the Empire had provided an opportunity for rioting; the Essenes and the Zealots were always quick to seize their chance.

So what were the Twelve contemplating behind my back? Peter now held sway over the small group of former activists, John, James, Simon and Iscariot. Embittered by poverty, this hot-headed fisherman seemed to want to get closer to our treasurer, who looked after the common purse with such scrupulous honesty. Were they thinking of taking action? Because there would never be a better moment than during this Passover, in the year 30. Was the fear that could be seen in their eyes prompted by the knowledge that there was going to be an attack on the Temple – and that like so many others, they were hoping for this at the same time as being afraid that it might end badly? Blood would be spilt, possibly their own.

I have often disagreed with them, and have sometimes berated them, while still continuing to love them – even tonight, when I know they have betrayed me. They are a reflection of the Jewish people itself, beside themselves with the anguish that they have had to bear for so long, the hopes that have been repeatedly dashed. But they have followed me all the way from Galilee, and since I didn't choose them, I have had to accept them as they are.

We had just come through Jericho, where I had been staying at the house of a wealthy tax collector by the name of Zacchaeus. Before us lay a great wilderness of sand and stones, in the distance beyond it a range of small mountains through which winds the narrow road that leads to Jerusalem, teetering here and there along the edge of canyons whose depth and severe beauty takes your breath away.

Jericho could never forget that it was the first oasis that Joshua captured, long before David made Jerusalem his capital. A proud town, it kept its distance from the vainglorious city of the Temple. It had its share of activists, although unlike those elsewhere they were less inclined to discriminate against people who worked for the inspectorate of taxes: since there was no escaping the scourge of the occupying forces, wasn't it better if the dirty work was done by one's fellow countrymen, provided they didn't line their pockets at the taxpayer's expense? Zacchaeus was such a man, so my presence in his house didn't attract any adverse comment.

As we were leaving the town a large crowd gathered round me, publicly defying Jerusalem's policy of suspicion towards me. There was a blind beggar who had taken up permanent residence at the roadside. Hearing the noise, he asked what was happening. When he was told that Jesus the Nazarene was passing by, he raised his sightless eyes to heaven and cried out at the top of his voice:

"Jesus, Son of David, have mercy on me!"

214

According to an old Jewish legend, David's son Solomon had possessed great powers of healing. With nothing else to hope for, the man suddenly remembered this and seized on it. People sternly told him to be quiet, but he shouted even louder: "Son of David!..." Touched by this reference to our shared heritage, I asked what his name was; he was called Bartimaeus, and lived shut away in eternal darkness. I told everyone to stop trying to make him keep quiet, and to let him come to me. When he heard my voice he leapt up, threw off his cloak and hurried over.

Bartimaeus seemed very excited, so I asked him:

"What do you want me to do for you?"

He immediately replied:

"*Rabbouni*, let me see again!"

Rabbouni, or "my little master": it was impossible to resist this affectionate diminutive. Was the man comparing me with Solomon? What did it matter? In his blindness he had called on God, so he was healed already. I told him so:

"Go; your faith has made you well."

Unable to believe that he had recovered his sight, he insisted on coming with me. But news of the healing had already spread around the oasis. As I made my way into the mountains, local activists went on ahead to tell the Zealots in Jerusalem. It was only right that the new Solomon should be given a fitting reception in the City of David.

As I climbed the steep-sided path, I thought about my healing of Bartimaeus. I think it was the first time I had ever said to a sick person, "What do you want *me to do* for you?" Coming to me, displaying his condition in public was an act of faith – but faith in *whom*? Every time I performed a healing I always followed it by saying something that made it clear that God alone was responsible. Yet they put their trust, as well as their lives, in the hands of the charismatic rabbi from Galilee – they had faith *in me*.

Should I spurn this personality cult? Bartimaeus had called me *rabbouni*: ought I to correct people when they used this name, with its emotionally charged overtones? I never dared. For them, being healed was the beginning of a new life; it was only later they would realize that this rebirth wasn't brought about by me.

As I suspected, when I came down into the Kidron Valley there was a little welcoming committee waiting for me. They insisted on performing a symbolic gesture, and had managed to find a donkey, which they sat me on, then tore armfuls of leafy branches from the trees and threw them in front of it. Urged on by the Zealots, the small crowd began shouting "Hosanna to the Son of David!" As always, up on the walls Roman legionaries were watching for the slightest activity among the crowd on the Temple esplanade – so you had to know just how far you could go. Deciding to call a halt to this public display that might provoke an armed response, I climbed off the donkey and the hotheads from Jericho went home. Without entering the city walls, my disciples and I walked along a dried-up stream bed that led to Bethany.

I had returned to Jerusalem for the last time.

44

When we were still a short way from the village, the Judaean came out to meet me. He had never left Lazarus's bedside, and told me that he had died four days earlier. So, our friend had slipped away at the very moment I was told he was ill! When I expressed my regret for not coming sooner, he said I shouldn't be sorry for healing Bartimaeus in Jericho – word of which had just reached Bethany, along with that of my so-called triumphal arrival at the gates of Jerusalem. He also said I was mad to come back to Jerusalem – Nicodemus and Joseph of Arimathea were keeping him up to date with the discussions that were going on in the Sanhedrin, who were looking for any excuse to have me arrested.

We walked on ahead, the Twelve some distance behind. I was expecting to find the house full of friends and hired mourners, acquaintances from Jerusalem where Lazarus had had many clients. All of a sudden Martha came rushing up to us, eyes red and hair covered in ashes. She stopped in front of me and chided me for not coming sooner – if only I had been there!

"I know that my brother will rise again in the resurrection on the last day," she said, holding back her tears.

Resurrection! That word! It leads us nowhere. It proves just how strong a hold death has over the minds of the Jewish people, to the extent where they believe it is something final. Standing in front of Martha, I searched her face, which was gaunt with grief. What could I say to release her from the straitjacket of Jewish beliefs? It wasn't the time or the place. I just mumbled:

"Your brother will rise again."

Without replying she hurried back to the house. I didn't want to go near the place, not now, when Lazarus was no longer in a home that he had filled with his lively, infectious warmth, to find Mary prostrate and surrounded by people trying to comfort her... But then she suddenly appeared, breathless from running, and knelt at my feet:

"Rabbi, if you had been here, my brother would not have died!"

Dear, sweet Mary! It was more than I could bear. I gave a shudder, struggling to hold back my tears. By now the crowd of friends, clients and official mourners had gathered round. To disguise my lack of composure, I asked them:

"Where have you laid him?"

"Rabbi, come and see..."

I looked round to ask my disciples to come with us, but they were nowhere in sight.

The tomb was in a cave cut into the rock on a slight slope. It was a rich man's burial chamber, as could be seen from the large circular stone that had been placed over the opening. Inside there would be a table, on which the body had been laid out after being anointed with precious lotions and perfumes. Like the Judaean, Lazarus had been an Essene; the body would shortly be moved to a side alcove, and then after a year the mortal remains would be exhumed. According to the rites of the Qumran community, the bones would be ceremonially washed in a final baptism, after which they would be reinterred in a permanent tomb, possibly in an Essene, not a Jewish cemetery – in untainted ground.

About a dozen paces from the entrance, the crowd suddenly halted: the same as entering a room where there is a dead body, to go near a tomb would render them unclean, a state that requires a week of purification, and the Passover was in six days' time. The lack of stress I place on the purity laws was well known – so would I go in? But I just took a step forward and went no farther, unable to contain my tears any longer. Behind me I heard people whispering, "See how he loved him!" But some of them said acrimoniously, "Could not he who opened the eyes of the blind man have kept this man from dying?"

Again a shiver ran through me. Tears like those I shed in the wilderness were now streaming down my face, blurring my vision. Yes, I had loved Lazarus dearly, as I did his sisters. Yes, like them I grieved at the sight of this stone, which to a detached observer represented an insurmountable barrier. For them, Lazarus was dead for ever... while for Martha there was still hope. The last day? Indeed so, but I had seen something else in the way she looked at me, heard it in her voice, as well as in Mary's unspoken plea. The two of them had often listened to me, and they believed that this *something else* was possible.

I turned to Martha and said: "Take away the stone!"

Hopes suddenly raised, she wanted to do what I said, except...

"Rabbi," she said, whispering in my ear, "already there is a stench because he has been dead for four days!"

Martha, Martha!... Death isn't like a piece of rotting meat, an oozing corpse! Death represents the ultimate victory for the Evil One and his deadly dance. What is the difference between being reborn from inner decay while you are still alive, or when your body has begun to decompose? You believe that life never ends, don't you Martha? So do I. Tell your servants to move the stone.

As they rolled away the heavy slab, the crowd shrunk back at the sickly smell that came from the tomb. I closed my eyes:

Abba, never do you allow our faith to be in vain... I cried in a loud voice:

"Lazarus, come out!"

As Lazarus staggered from the tomb, still wrapped in winding bandages, the crowd gave a gasp of terror. Like so many birds, some of them took flight, and I told the others to help this living man to unbind himself from the very thing that still bound them to what lay deep inside them.

Preceded by the crowd, in its midst a Lazarus who was still unsteady on his feet, I strolled back to the house with the Judaean. He said that among those who had fled from the tomb he had seen one or two Sadducees. As far as they were concerned, what they had witnessed could only have been a resurrection, the very thought of which filled them with disgust – so much so that they wouldn't allow it to be discussed in Jerusalem. Why were they in such a hurry to get away, if not to tell the Sanhedrin? The Judaean often went to Caiaphas's palace, and had contacts there whom he could call on at any time of the day or night. My name was apparently on everyone's lips; I had to leave Jerusalem immediately.

Then Martha came over, her face wreathed with joy. To celebrate her brother being restored, she wanted to give a dinner party that evening and make it open house – I simply had to be there.

A feast to mark a rebirth... Martha, I wouldn't miss it for the world. You want to give a party for Lazarus and his friends that will reflect well on your household? But what I have in mind is a feast to celebrate the coming of the Kingdom. And tonight, you will give us a foretaste of that Kingdom.

It will hide the smell of death that hangs round the Evil One.

45

The main dining room had been specially decorated, the tables laid out in a U shape according to the Roman custom which had been adopted by well-to-do Jews. When I arrived I saw Lazarus, now bathed and dressed in his finest robes, sitting among a crowd of people I didn't know. He gestured me to sit on his left, the place of honour. As I made my way round the table I saw Judas and my disciples standing by the wall.

After the chanting of the Ritual Blessings, I and the other guests reclined on couches to have our feet washed, as tradition required. Mary came over to me, followed by a servant carrying a bowl of water. To my amazement she produced a small casket, opened it and held it out to me with a smile: it was full of a thick ointment, whose heavy smell was similar to the one that had come from Lazarus's tomb. She had used this costly balm to anoint her brother's lifeless body, and once she had washed my feet she began rubbing it on them.

As Martha served dinner, the house was filled with the fragrance of the perfume.

How quick you are to see, Mary... you don't say much, you listen. Among all the people who walked back to the house with us, you were the only one who heard the Judaean's warning, apart from him you are the only one to appreciate the danger that confronts the man who saved your brother. As a sign of your eternal gratitude you are anointing him with perfume – an honorary gesture much used by the people of the East. But as you lean over me, are you thinking that it might soon be my dead body that you will have to embalm?

From behind us I heard Judas mutter: "Why was this perfume not sold?" It must have cost as much as a year's wages for a labourer, so why wasn't the money given to the poor?

This was the former Sicarius talking – with the cry for social justice that this offshoot of the Zealots likes to make their watchword – as well as the honest treasurer. You couldn't really reproach him for it. But this was the first time since he joined the Twelve that he had criticized me openly – so what was on his mind?

I turned to him:

"You always have the poor with you! But me…"

No, you won't always have me.

At daybreak the next morning, the Judaean went off to find out what was happening. Caiaphas had called an emergency late-night session of the Sanhedrin, which Nicodemus had attended. The Council listened to a series of witnesses, and when they heard the description of events at the tomb, the Sadducees were unanimous in protesting about this magic trick that would only reinforce people's belief in resurrection. They then exchanged insults with the Pharisees, and Caiaphas had had to call them to order so the other witnesses could be heard.

The accounts of the celebratory dinner united them in a shared sense of outrage. All the witnesses spoke of the vast crowd of Jews who had come to the house in an endless cortège, not only because I was there but to see Lazarus risen from the dead. Forgetting their long-standing hatred for each other, the Pharisees and

Sadducees eventually managed to agree that it was vital to put an end to my activities.

"What are we to do? This man is performing many signs. If we let him go on like this, everyone will believe in him, and the Romans will come and destroy both our Holy Place and our nation!"

Then Caiaphas got up and spoke in his capacity as High Priest:

"You know nothing at all! You do not understand that it is better for you to have one man die for the people than to have the whole nation destroyed!"

In the end, reasons of State prevailed over petty infighting – what was the son of a country carpenter worth compared with the safety of the Jewish people as a whole? He had the majority behind him: I had to die.

Only Nicodemus had defended me against the rest. Ever the good Pharisee, he pointed out that Jewish case law requires the facts to be fully established and then judgement pronounced after hearing both parties.

"Our Law does not judge people without first giving them a hearing to find out what they have done, does it?"

But he was confronted by a vengeful mob. This Jesus was nothing but a village Pharisee, was there a single respected figure from his area who had any faith in him? Surely Nicodemus wasn't from Galilee as well was he, that breeding ground for everything associated with Zealotry? If he looked closer, he would find that no prophet had ever come from that part of the country.

When in the pale light of dawn Nicodemus told the Judaean about the meeting, he was still quivering with rage. The Council of the Sanhedrin had eventually decided to issue an arrest warrant: anyone who knew my whereabouts was to inform the authorities. And, since it was due to this resurrection that they were losing public support, Lazarus would have to die too!

After which they all went home, very pleased with their night's work.

The Judaean was aghast. Lazarus would be protected by his wealth and personal connections, he said. But me, a little rabbi who was just one of the common people – whom the Pharisees in Jerusalem regarded as no more than a rabble who lived in ignorance of the Law – from now on I would have to stay hidden, and stop coming and going as I pleased.

As he was talking, the Twelve gathered round, terrified. They were willing to follow an up-and-coming rabbi, but not a fugitive. In Galilee I had had no difficulty in galvanizing the crowds – so where were my supporters now? I had gradually turned everyone against me. First the Essenes, by criticizing their edict of hatred towards their enemies. Then Herod, whose police were on my trail. Then the Zealots, who after the scandal at the Temple believed that I was one of them – but what did I do yesterday? Fail to take advantage of their official welcome at the gates of Jerusalem. And now today I had been condemned to death by the highest authority in Israel before I had even done anything. So did I regard these dignitaries who wanted to have me killed as *my neighbours* too?

What reason did they have to follow me now? For some fanciful notion of a Kingdom that was a long way off, yet which had somehow arrived? For a theoretical feast with an *Abba* that no Jew had ever heard of?

But what frightened them more than the physical danger was that they might have misjudged me; that I had misled them.

It was then I noticed that Judas was standing with Peter.

Without a moment's hesitation I decided to take the Judaean's advice. Not far from here, in the village of Ephraim, there was a small community of Essenes. Their comrades at Qumran had helped me survive when I was in the wilderness, and one of them had told me that they could tell by my reasoning that I was a man after their own heart. So perhaps those at Ephraim could provide me with a breathing space for a few hours?

For the second time in my life my path would lead me to the Sons of Light.

46

I spent the night praying on the sand, while my disciples slept – yes, already.

Wherever I went from now on, I would be an outcast. In Galilee, Herod's police would soon pick up my trail. In Jerusalem and the surrounding area, the Sanhedrin's arrest warrant would never be far behind. Every human being is born to die – but as soon as I decided to follow in the footsteps of John the Baptist and then take on the mantle of Elijah, I was born to be killed. Yet our basic instincts refuse to accept this fact, and do all they can to avoid it. Would I have to leave my native land and go and live in the Jewish Diaspora in Antioch or Alexandria? To forget that when he decides to follow the special calling of his people to the very end, no Jew is ever *ordinary*?

Why us Jews? Why me? If I had asked the One whom no one is permitted to question – as Job discovered to his cost – it would have choked off the silence that was struggling to rise up out of the darkness.

For at that moment, more than anything I needed silence.

By the time the first rays of dawn were lighting up the horizon, I had come to a decision: the journey that began when I left the family workshop in Capernaum to go and listen to the Baptist's gruff voice would end in Jerusalem. A Jew accepts death, but he is forbidden actively to seek it out; I wasn't intending to commit suicide, I would do everything I could not to be caught – or at least, not too soon. Not before I had played the final note of a symphony that had been composed by Someone other than me.

As a devout Jew, I knew I could seek refuge in the palm of his hand, this Other. It was into his hands that I commended my spirit, my life, my soul.

So on a bright sunny morning in Judaea I set off on the road to Jerusalem. Followed by my disciples – but for how much longer?

Since Lazarus could expect to avoid the consequences of his "resurrection" due to his position in society, I went straight to his house at Bethany to find him. I was soon joined by the Judaean, who, being less prominent than Nicodemus, was able to come and go more easily. There were things we had to discuss.

Lazarus was the first to ask me a question that must have been bothering him ever since he started to follow – albeit from a distance – my short-lived career: why on earth had I taken such an extreme line over everything? I told him quite sharply that I hadn't been extreme, except perhaps in putting compassion before all ideological belief. To fight Evil is to refuse to admit defeat when faced with human suffering, whatever its cause and in whatever shape or form it appears. And I went on to say that it was Judaism that is extreme, because it only acknowledges One God among all the different deities in the world, and one Law out of the vast array of legal systems used by the human race. If I had broken the Law, it was in order to stretch it to its limit. Was taking the intuition of the prophets all the way to this limit, where it sinks into the silence of God, the behaviour of an extremist?

"So the life you lead is that of a prophet?" said Lazarus.

Does any life have a precise trajectory? Was I able to define mine by what I was? Or, like the vast majority of people, by what I had failed to be? My life couldn't be defined in terms of its actions; I was asking my friends to judge it by the powerful intuition that had been its driving force ever since I left the family home.

"In that case," said Lazarus, with a note of finality, "you know what you have to do. A prophet never ceases to prophesy; it is only Jerusalem that is able to silence his voice."

The Judaean took a more businesslike approach. On the day that I went into hiding in the village of Ephraim, he had walked round the Temple esplanade, listening to gossip. Everyone was wondering if I would show myself during the Passover, which was in four days' time. Some people were saying: "Surely he won't come to the festival, will he?" He had detected a tremendous sense of expectation among the crowds, one that was shared by my disciples — which is probably why they stayed with me in spite of everything. Yet he was wary of them, and felt they represented as much of a risk to me as did the members of the Sanhedrin. When I dismissed this suggestion he pulled me up short — it might just be that he had a clearer idea of what was going on in their minds than I did at the moment. And he went on to say (in terms I didn't really understand at the time) that his main concern was to protect me from their political ambitions.

So I had to make a decision. I couldn't stay with Lazarus, although as long as I moved around among the throng of pilgrims I would be untouchable – the Jewish police would never dare arrest me on the Temple esplanade, which is where fugitives from justice usually seek sanctuary.

So I would spend the day in the shadows beneath the pillars that run along the esplanade of Solomon, while in the evenings I would slip back quietly to the safety of the oil press in the Garden of Gethsemane at the foot of the Mount of Olives, which looks out over the Temple. No Jew would dare venture there at night because of the tombs that are dotted all over the Kidron Valley, which would cause them to become unclean if they strayed too close to them in the darkness.

One question remained: what of the Passover? How and where would we be able to celebrate the festival of Jewish national identity? The custom for poorer families is to club together to buy a lamb that is ritually slaughtered the day before in the Temple, which is transformed into a vast abattoir for the occasion. The carcass is then collected by one of the families, who invite their neighbours to share the meat before sitting down to a private celebratory dinner. Even wealthy people share, for this is part of the tradition – a Jew never spends the Passover away from his own kind.

It was out of the question for me openly to share the paschal lamb with Lazarus's family and neighbours. So what were we to do?

The Judaean thought for a moment, then made a suggestion. Of all the different factions that existed in Israel, the Essenes were the ones I had treated with the most sensitivity. My criticism of them had always been oblique, and in many of the ways we chose to live, my disciples and I felt close to them – so why not celebrate as they did? Ever since they had been with me, my disciples had followed my example and stopped sacrificing in the Temple. A meal without lamb – which although not truly paschal was still solemn and sacramental – would make us feel part of the people of Moses as they commemorated the crossing of the Red Sea.

As for where… The safest place would be his house, since it was in the western part of the city, home to many prominent people and Caiaphas's palace, which was closely guarded by the Jewish police. No one would think of looking for us there.

I straight away agreed, and thanked the Judaean for being brave enough to invite us to his home. He said that one of his servants

THE SILENCE OF GETHSEMANE

carrying a water jar would meet us, and lead us through this afflu-
ent neighbourhood, where we had never set foot before. Without
that, our appearance and Galilean accents would soon give us away.

When I left Lazarus's house I wanted to tell my disciples, but
once again they were nowhere to be seen. By now it was getting
dark. Keeping to the shadows on the outside of the city wall, I
made my way to the Garden of Gethsemane.

Alone.

47

My disciples joined me later, guided by Judas, who knew a route that avoided the tombs, and we settled down for the night as the Passover moon rose higher in the sky.

There were three days left before the start of the festival – three days that now seem like a lifetime, yet which went by like a whirlwind. The next morning there were so many people around the Temple that I didn't feel at all anxious as I walked up the colossal entrance steps: the police wouldn't take any notice of a pilgrim in a well-made coat because they were looking for a fugitive dressed in rags. Yet as soon as people realized I was there, they came at me in a great tide to try and make me say something, just as a bull is stunned before the fatal blow is struck. I had always thought that I was the one on the attack, but now I had to hold my position every inch of the way.

It was the Sadducees in their tall hats who led the charge. They were aware that, like Hillel, I had said there was life after death – although unlike him I described the afterlife in some detail as a kingly feast. They referred to the passage in the Law that says that if a Jew's brother dies leaving a wife but no children, he has a duty to marry the widow. In unctuous tones they asked: if the eldest of seven brothers dies and leaves no children, does the second-eldest brother not have to marry his widow? But if the second brother also dies, and likewise all of the remaining brothers, none of them leaving children... then according to my teaching about the resurrection on the Last Day, of all the brothers whose wife will she be – because all seven have married her one after another?

Theologians! Wasn't it typical of them to split hairs! As the crowd stood listening, I replied calmly and unhurriedly. To be resurrected doesn't mean coming back to life in the same body and with the same desires although in different climes. The proof could be found in those I had healed, who had each been recreated as a new person, not just a resurrection of the old one; similar to their original self, but no longer dancing to Evil's tune. This is what the simpleton in Capernaum and all the others had experienced, a sensation of euphoria at being cured. I explained that when we are reborn on the Last Day we will be like the angels in heaven, of whom we know nothing except that they stand rejoicing in the presence of God for all eternity.

As for the Law...

"Have you not read in the book of Moses, in the story about the Burning Bush, how God said to him: '*I am the God of Abraham, the God of Isaac and the God of Jacob*'? He is God not of the dead, but of the living."

Faced with these men wearing the insignia of their power, and who regarded God as their personal property, I thought back to my time in the wilderness, which was much like Moses's experience at the Burning Bush. And I told them that they were quite wrong – for at the top of Mount Sinai, the Law was set in stone. But in the presence of the God of loving kindness it takes on new life, trampling down death for ever. There is no more death; my God is the God of the living.

Once again I insisted that my source lay in the origins of the Law, in the story of the Patriarchs.

Among the audience I recognized the Scribe who had once asked me about the order in which the commandments should be placed. He had been listening carefully, and smiled at me before walking away, telling anyone who cared to listen that I had answered well. In public, the Sadducees and the Scribes avoided locking horns with each other like they do in the Council; the bemitred men took no notice of him, and just disappeared. Here I was protected by the crowd, who were delighted to see me stand up to them.

In Galilee I had always sensed that I was talking to the majority, the Judaism into which I was born. What set my teaching apart was that it was based on the belief that opposites could co-exist and didn't cancel each other out: thus the familiarity of the word *Abba* was not an act of lese-majesty towards the Father Almighty, nor did the law of the heart negate the commandments. I wasn't abolishing anything (except for hypocritical oaths and barbaric divorce laws), I was helping the flower of Judaism to bring forth its finest fruit. But this wasn't the place for such subtle distinctions: you had to be on one side or the other or keep quiet.

But during the night I spent at Ephraim, I had decided not to keep quiet.

By blending in with the crowd I managed to get back to the Garden of Gethsemane. I found my disciples standing on the slope, gazing at the great edifice of the Temple in the light of the setting sun.

"Look, Rabbi," they said, "what large stones, what large buildings!"

My mind still full of the altercation with the Sadducees, I just mumbled that it was nothing, that it would all be cast down eventually. Peter and the Boanerges brothers immediately took me aside. With conspiracy written all over their faces they asked me what I knew, if the end was approaching, if I was going to give the sign that everyone was waiting for.

There was nothing I could say. If they were so incensed with destroying the Temple then why not do so, another one would only take its place, if not in Jerusalem then somewhere else. Who knows, they might be the ones to lay the foundation stones personally. The Temple of God, however, was them themselves – but they were prevented from entering it by the great gates of their ambition.

I looked round for Iscariot. So where was Judas?

48

In Galilee, Roman legionaries were few and far between, but in Judaea their constant presence helped keep the nationalists' feelings of hatred alive as if rubbing salt into a wound. After the events of the last two days, I had to wait until the next morning before I was asked for my opinion about the laws that were imposed by the occupying power, the way it governed and plundered the country.

The first shots were fired by a group of Herod's minor officials, who were used for low-level intelligence-gathering in Galilee. I was surprised to see them keeping company with prominent Pharisees. Was it mere coincidence that these natural enemies happened to be there at the same time, or had they joined forces in order to try and entrap me, knowing the crowd of pilgrims in Jerusalem was swarming with Zealots?

They took the same sly, ingratiating approach as the Sadducees the day before.

"Rabbi, we know that you are sincere and show deference to no one; for you do not regard people with partiality, but teach the way of God in accordance with truth…"

Beneath the honeyed words and the deep, exaggerated bows, I detected the poisoned arrow.

"Tell us: is it lawful to pay taxes to Caesar, yes or no?"

The barb went deep. As well as indirect taxation, the various provinces under Roman rule have to pay a set tax imposed on colonies. In the year 12, the nationalists had rebelled against this tribute, which is like a shameful brand burnt into the flesh of the Jews, while the Zealots forbid their followers to pay it at all. To answer "yes" would be to defend the Roman occupation and thus alienate myself from the only nation in the world who stubbornly refuses to submit to it, and make enemies of the fanatical supporters of independence as well as the silent majority who are secretly on their side. To say "no" would mean being immediately arrested by Roman soldiers.

The Pharisees in Galilee had already heard me denounce the practice of oath-taking, and describe the basis for a non-religious partnership between the sacred and the secular. But now I was confronted with senior members of both the clerical and civil authorities, who always make common cause when it comes to safeguarding their privileges. I asked to see a coin of the kind used to pay taxes.

"Whose head is this on it, and whose title?"

"Caesar's!" they answered with one voice.

"In that case," I said, "give to Caesar what is Caesar's, and to God what is God's!"

In the space of a few words I had managed to unite the entire esplanade against me. The Zealots, who were furious that I had defended the tax on colonies – as if the land of Israel belonged to Caesar! The Herodians, offended that I had publicly reminded everyone that they only paid lip service to God. The senior clergy in Jerusalem, who would never allow the religious and civil authorities to be separated. And last but not least the mob, among them my disciples, who were disappointed as well as outraged that I hadn't taken a stand against Rome in the name of mystical beliefs that they neither understood nor shared.

The mass of people moved away, leaving me in the open, and a group of Scribes took advantage of my sudden isolation. Of all the Pharisees, these thinkers are the most dangerous; when they saw them appear, the crowd gathered round again. The Scribes asked if I believed that the long-awaited Messiah was the son of David.

It was a particularly shrewd and underhand question, which in a sense encapsulated everything that they held against me. Hadn't there been whisperings in Galilee (and not just among my disciples) that I might be the Messiah? Didn't other people say that the Messiah was the son of God, by whom the divine presence is maintained on earth? Whatever the case, if the Messiah were the son of David – the priest-king – didn't that prove that the civil and religious powers in Israel could never be taken in isolation?

Faced with these past masters in the art of pedantry, there was only one way to answer such a multifaceted question: by referring to the sacred text. Speaking over their heads to the crowd behind them, I said:

"How can the Scribes say that the Messiah is the son of David?"

In one of his Psalms, which all my listeners would be familiar with, doesn't David himself speak to God and call him *Lord*? So how could he be his son?

Although I don't think the crowd appreciated the finer points of the argument, they were always quick to show their delight whenever the little rabbi from Galilee put members of the supreme authority in their place. As previously with the wealthy young man, I had stated quite plainly that I was not the son of God. Now cheated of the main reason for levelling a charge against me, that of blasphemy, which was punishable by death, the assault receded. One or two of them came over and quietly congratulated me for giving such a good answer.

When they had gone I was left alone among the crowd; my disciples were nowhere to be seen.

Yet I had created this distance intentionally. Down through the ages, the prophets of Israel have railed against the slave trade, the barbarity of the various Jewish dynasties, their handling of public affairs, the exploitation of the poor. I had never done this, and in some of my parables I even seemed to treat the unbridled capitalism that holds sway in Israel as a fact of life. This was because I never claimed to be trying to change the world, or to prevent it from dancing with Evil.

I wanted to *proclaim its end*.

What of money? It was king, and would remain so – but my Kingdom was of another kind. To believe – as my disciples did – that the world could be transformed by the use of violence would only perpetuate the diabolic spell that the Evil One casts in order to set one man against another.

I wanted to break this spell by wresting the world out of Satan's clutches, by proclaiming that we would no longer dance to his tune. For me there are no more secrets lurking in the deepest depths of the shadows – the Evil One is no longer the prince of darkness, the light must shine on Man and his domain.

And then I cast a new spell, using parables to restore the power that our imagination has over harsh reality. By making nature the stage on which life is lived, it ceased to be a dark corner full of religious suspicion. I transformed it into something poetic, something that sings of the highest truths.

Instead of allowing it mysteriously to fuel people's desire for violence of all kinds, I used the imagination as the driving force of my Kingdom.

Yet here on the Temple esplanade, I was able to judge the full extent of my failure. My disciples would have accepted sweeping changes to their faith – but instead of a new creed I had painted pictures for them. I hadn't condemned their Judaism, I had invited them to take the dangerous path of freedom. The Judaean was right: not only were they incapable of hearing my message, but their disillusionment would lead them in only one direction – the betrayal of their rabbi.

49

The next morning was today. At first light I set off for the Temple. The Judaean was waiting for me on the path that runs beside the dried-up floor of the Kidron Valley. He said that he had spent the previous day in the city but hadn't witnessed my altercation with the various worthies – but he had got wind of it. At that very moment, the Sanhedrin were trying to turn the politically active elements of the populace against me. That was why they had asked me about the tax paid by colonies, and my ambivalent response had given them cause to rejoice: as well as the devout Jews, who were outraged by my pronouncements on divorce and love, the nationalists were now distancing themselves from the inconstant rabbi who didn't seem able to lead an all-out revolt. Having once enjoyed popular support, I now found myself isolated.

"What of the Twelve?" I asked.

He said they didn't have the means to lead an assault on the Temple, nor was it their ambition. The Zealots were always poised to do so, however; when they left the Temple esplanade the day before, the former activists among my disciples – led by Peter – had managed to persuade them that rather than pushing me into the background they would do better to use my popularity to gain the support of as many ordinary people as possible. Three of them – the Barjona, Simon the Zealot and Iscariot – had each been promptly issued with a *sica*, the short sword that gives its name to the Sicarii, who use them to disembowel their enemies. For his part, he admitted to feeling uneasy: if they did use force, he said, then like all the previous occasions there would be a bloodbath, and I would be killed before anyone had a chance to arrest me. Whereas if I were to be tried by the Sanhedrin, where we had friends (such as Nicodemus and Joseph of Arimathea), and where he also had contacts, I would stand a good chance.

So what did he suggest?

His face drawn and haggard, he said he had something in mind, not without risk, but it was the only thing he could think of given the situation. This very morning he was due to see Judas and was going to try and talk him round; he couldn't tell me any more than that – except that I should avoid drawing attention to myself on the Temple esplanade today, and not get involved in any public debates. The upper room of his house in the western part of the city would be ready for us that evening as arranged; he had instructed one of his servants to meet us carrying a jar of water. In the meantime I should do my best to keep out of sight.

For some time I was alone in the empty valley. The Twelve... I had been glad to have Peter and his brother Andrew with me, as well as John and his brother James, who were the first ones to join me. After them came others, who gave up everything to follow me... Everything, that is, except their illusions; everything except that typical Jewish disquiet which helped keep their wild expectations alive. They listened to me proclaim the end of one world and the beginning of a new one – they listened, but they didn't hear. Yet I couldn't hold this against them; there has been far too much suffering in Israel for far too long, and they were the repository of all that. From the moment I ceased to share their disquiet, we had gone our separate ways. They weren't dreaming up a base act of betrayal, of that I was convinced: a disciple never betrays his rabbi. So what was on their minds?

Judas... scrupulously honest Judas, who had been drawn to the Sicarii with their unsubtle, summary ideals! Of all my disciples he is the only one with whom I willingly exchange kisses, the only one whom I occasionally refer to as my *hetairos*, or companion. He isn't a close friend in the same sense as Lazarus, but someone I trust. So why does the Judaean want to speak to him today? I can't imagine for a moment that the highly respectable, refined city dweller and this poor, down-to-earth activist could be in league with each other. Yet what they do have in common is their love of Israel, as well as affection for me. I have never had any doubts about what Judas feels — he is someone who wears his heart on his sleeve. Peter is more complex, however, and all the more unfathomable because his liking for power and violence has so far never found an outlet.

When I arrived there was a sizeable crowd on the Temple esplanade. Wishing to avoid confrontations, I stood where the swarming mass of pilgrims was at its thickest, near the treasury where people come to make offerings. They were queuing up at the barrel-like container, where the loose change made a ringing sound as it tumbled in. I spotted some of my disciples and gestured to them. Peter walked over, followed by the others, attracted by the sight of the rich people pulling back the sleeves of their robes so everyone could see the handfuls of gold coins that they jingled before tossing them into the treasury.

Money! It was the tangible sign of their failure, of an affluence and power from which they would always be excluded! They were staring at the pile of gold and copper as if bewitched when a little old woman came up, almost as if trying not to be seen. She was wearing a widow's veil, and slipped in two lepta, the smallest denomination of coin. I turned to my disciples and said:

"Truly I tell you, this poor widow has put in more than all the others. For all of them have contributed out of their abundance, but she out of her poverty has put in everything she had to live on."

They said not a word. While we were in Galilee I had told them my opinion of money on several occasions – that there is nothing wrong with it when it is used to serve the interests of humanity, but not those of power. This woman was worth more than all these rich people put together, probably more than the priests to whom her two small coins would be given.

But they weren't listening, any more than they had in Galilee. Reflected in their eyes I saw the glitter of gold.

By now it was late in the day. I arranged to meet them where the Judaean's servant carrying a water jar would come and find us, to guide us through the western part of the city.

I was going to hear the outcome of the negotiations that the Judaean had had with Judas that morning.

And perhaps what fate has in store for me tonight.

50

The ordinary Essenes who live in towns and cities are not able to observe the rite of baptism by immersion before meals as is the custom at Qumran, so instead they purify their whole body, or as much as is practical. Although fetching water is deemed woman's work, this was why the man walking in front of us carrying a large container of water didn't attract attention. People recognized him as one of the Judaean's staff; his master – who was known to have been a member of the sect – was probably holding a traditional Essene dinner, for which he would need a great deal of water.

The servant took us by a roundabout route, so as not to pass the police detachments outside Caiaphas's palace and the homes of various dignitaries. Like most of the houses in this part of town, our host's had a large function room that took up an entire floor. The Judaean met us at the bottom of the stairs, and gestured to the Twelve to go up and finish getting the room ready: he obviously wanted to talk to me.

In a hushed voice, he told me that the Zealots now had high hopes of achieving their insane ambition to take the Temple by storm. Nicodemus had told him that the Sanhedrin were aware of this; it was the same every year during Passover. Steps had been taken, several cohorts of Roman legionaries were on standby, the whole enterprise would be nipped in the bud, and the ringleaders would have their throats cut before they could whip up support from the populace.

He confirmed his earlier suspicions that my disciples had allowed themselves to be taken in by this madness. So he had decided to pre-empt them: that morning he had managed to persuade Judas to go with him into the inner recesses of the High Priest's palace to negotiate with him to have me arrested before any riots could break out. Trials weren't allowed during the Passover, so if something happened in the meantime, having me safely under lock and key would prove I was innocent. On Monday I would appear before the Council of the Sanhedrin, who would have no choice but to make it a matter of record that I couldn't have been involved in any mob violence. I might be flogged and then released, having been formally forbidden to teach in Jerusalem. This is the normal procedure, and his friends on the Council would ensure that it was followed.

So what had Judas said?

He had agreed. Have his rabbi arrested and kept in a safe place before rioting started? Iscariot had eventually come round to his way of thinking, even seemed relieved. But at the same time he wanted a formal undertaking from the High Priest that at no time would my life be in danger. Caiaphas had smiled and produced a purse from beneath his cloak: he took a solemn oath before God that I would be spared the death penalty. And then, in accordance with legal practice in Israel, he had given Iscariot thirty pieces of silver, instead of the fifty prescribed by the Law. This was the price he charged for swearing, on pain of anathema, not to have a man of low birth put to death.

His mind now at rest, Judas had taken the silver, which effectively sealed the agreement between himself and the High Priest in the presence of God. Since he always knew where to find me, he would be able to lead the Temple police to me at a propitious moment, and out of sight of the crowds, so everything would go smoothly.

My heart was pounding. "So... when will it be?" I mumbled.

For the first time the Judaean looked me in the eye: it would be one night before the end of the celebrations, so I could be tried on Monday morning. And if the Temple police refused to arrest someone during the religious festival, then soldiers from one of the cohorts would simply do it instead. He would meet us in Gethsemane every evening from now on, so he could make sure everything went according to plan. After my arrest he would follow me to the inner courtyard of the High Priest's palace, where he knew the gatekeeper.

I was horrified. So was this how my career would end? Arrested under cover of darkness, locked up in the High Priest's palace then silenced... I looked the Judaean in the eye: he had followed his conscience, I had to trust him. But there was one thing I had to ask: from what he knew, was it the Twelve who had *betrayed me*?

He didn't have to think before answering. Judas? Yes, to start with he had undoubtedly lent Peter a sympathetic ear. But by agreeing to play a part in my arrest he had helped to wreck any plans that Barjona and the Zealots were making. His affection for me, his deep-seated loyalty to the rabbi who trusted him, as well as his devout Jew's instinctive mistrust of Peter's violent nature, had swung him away from the activist cause at the last minute.

And Peter? It was clear he wanted to use me to win over the masses once the coup had taken place. For the last few days, he had done nothing but talk – quite openly – about the kingdom I had promised to create once Israel finally showed signs of rebelling, and the role that various individuals would play in it. He must have believed that by acting in this way he was being true to the ideals of the entire nation. The hard core of activists among the Twelve supported him, but the others were apparently unaware of what he was hatching.

With a sad smile he gestured to me to go upstairs.

How could things have come to this? When they had left everything to follow me, they had been filled with genuine fervour. They had loved me, I was quite certain of that. So what had I done to make all that passion suddenly evaporate?

I was about to eat a formal, celebratory supper with the very people who were betraying me.

And I was going to have to dip my hand in the same dish as them.

51

It was no more than a few hours ago, I should be able to remember every detail quite easily, yet nothing will come back to me. It is as if everything in that upper room were somehow unreal, as if every word that was spoken there took on another meaning, the slightest gesture assumed a significance quite different from what it seemed to represent.

Peter, James and John? Ever since we have been together I have known that they formed a clique, and there were times when I showed favouritism towards this alliance by treating them as a separate group. Then when James and John demanded the best positions for themselves, they split up. Yet despite their differences of opinion, Peter is no longer just one of the disciples – he is the leader of a faction that is involved in a plot.

Tonight, they all believe that Judas is still part of this conspiracy. They have no reason to doubt him, no way of knowing that this very morning he deceived them by making a secret agreement with Caiaphas.

And Judas? At the last moment he has been persuaded to betray the betrayers. He knows his life is in danger – if Peter discovers what happened he will never forgive him, he will be found in an alleyway somewhere in the Old Town, with his belly slit open and his intestines scattered far and wide.

What of the Judaean?... If his plan succeeds, his social position will protect him from Peter and the Boanerges brothers, although not from their hatred, which will know no bounds. And if Caiaphas breaks his word, then my supporters will blame him and Judas for my death.

Unlike the others in the room, I will keep faith with my true, inner self. But I will have to go along with the pretence as well. I am choked with fear and sadness.

Lined up along the wall, in front of the cushions that have been laid out in a U shape, they are waiting for me: twelve men, the bearers of hopes and secrets cloaked in lies.

They had all left their coats on a low table just inside the door. As I came in I noticed the handles of three *sicas* protruding from the folds; they belonged to Peter, Judas and Simon the Zealot. So the Judaean was telling the truth: they were armed.

For me, every celebratory supper in Galilee had always been a reflection of the Kingdom that was to come. When I saw the Twelve I decided that this meal would be no different; like all the others it would be a symbolic feast; I would just have to ignore the bad atmosphere, the weapons that were left at the door. The Essene customs that we were using would make things easier: I would take the place of the priest and celebrate, as was the practice at Qumran.

After the chanting of the Ritual Blessings, the Judaean settled himself in the middle, gesturing to me to sit on his left. The custom is to prop yourself up on your left elbow when eating; to his right, where space had been left for the staff to serve, he had a side-on view of Peter's face and shoulder.

The dishes were placed in front of us. Hillel always made it clear that if a Jew doesn't eat the Passover lamb, he cuts himself off from the body of Israel. They were aware of this, and listened with solemn faces as I pronounced the blessing that spoke of the unshakeable unity of God's Chosen People.

The time came for the rite of baptism. I got up from the table, took off my outer robe and tied a towel round my waist as is customary. Then, pouring water into a basin brought by the man who had led us to the house, I began to wash my disciples' feet and wipe them with the towel.

The room went quiet. When I came to Peter he stiffened, and, speaking for the first time since the meal began, he burst out:

"Rabbi, are you going to wash my feet?"

What did he mean? That by taking the place of an Essene priest I was laying claim to a role and a status to which I wasn't entitled? Acting on impulse as usual, he had spoken without thinking. So I replied:

"You do not know now what I am doing, but later you will understand."

"You will never wash my feet!"

Was he objecting to the future king of Israel behaving submissively, refusing to be served by someone whom he expected to share power with? I wanted to know.

"Unless I wash you, you have no share with me."

"Rabbi, not my feet only but also my hands and my head!"

Weighed down by mysteries that were impenetrable to him, he clung to the idea of the cool, clear water that he had first known when John the Baptist baptized him in the River Jordan. He had experienced this act of purification with the open-handed candour of the newly converted. I reminded him of this:

"One who has bathed entirely does not need to have his feet washed, but is entirely clean."

We were looking into each other's eyes, our faces were a hand's breadth apart. The time had come to make it clear that I wasn't taken in, that he was dancing to the Evil One's tune. I stared at him, and he stared back.

"And you are clean, but not all of you!"

I hurled this thinly disguised accusation in his face as I knelt in front of him, not Judas. So now he knew: I had uncovered his secret.

Without another word I moved on to the next person.

I went back to my place to give the usual homily. What could I say to them, these men who had followed me without ever really catching up? I wanted to leave them a form of legacy. So even if they had failed to understand me, they could at least remember our long journeys together, the compassion I had always shown for people with no fixed roots, my boundless patience with those who opposed me. I had never wanted to be served, simply to serve, to bathe the wounds that Evil had inflicted on them. I ended my address on a sorrowful note:

"For I have set you an example, that you also should do as I have done to you."

It was the last time I would be a rabbi teaching his disciples.

52

After that the meal continued in heavy silence. Everyone kept their eyes on their food, closed off within themselves.

When the moment came for the sharing of the bread, the image of mealtimes in the family home in Capernaum suddenly came flooding back to me, everyone talking quietly round the table, those gentle childhood moments that never leave us. Joseph would bless the loaf, then with a smile our mother would give a piece to each of us children in turn, smile at us with an expression of affection that was quite unforgettable... the unexpected memory sent a tremor of emotion through my whole being – so were the Twelve plotting against me? Was I surrounded by turncoats? My mind plunged in turmoil, I had to know. Breaking the round, flat loaf as they looked on, I said:

"Take; this is my body which is given."

Because I was looking down at the bread, I didn't see who started the whisper that was soon running round the table. The word *given* could be taken to mean two things, either *given* or *given up*. I overheard some of them ask the person next to them why I had replaced the usual blessing with this obscure pronouncement. Now they would have to declare themselves; slowly I poured wine into the cup.

"Take, drink, this is my blood, poured out for many."

There was an immediate outcry. Was I saying that I was going to be *given up* like a common criminal, that my blood would flow like wine?

I kept my eye on Peter, Judas and the Boanerges brothers: they were the only ones saying nothing, as if turned to stone, while the others were shifting in their seats and demanding to know what I meant. But I didn't get a chance to reply – the unambiguous reference to my imminent death roused the demon of their old ambitions, the endless bickering over power. They began hurling insults at each other across the table; if I were no longer there, who would take my place?

Amid the uproar, Peter and his friends seemed to have been struck dumb. But their silence provided the answer to my question: the others seemed genuinely surprised, their obvious display of disunity showed they knew nothing of any conspiracy.

They weren't conniving against me.

Peter!

I was so shocked that I only managed to utter:

"Truly I tell you, one of you will betray me."

A deathly silence descended on the room. They looked round at each other, wondering whom I meant. Then Peter turned to the person on his left. Still speechless, he gestured to him to ask me what I knew.

The Judaean leant towards me, his head almost on my shoulder, and whispered:

"Who is it, Rabbi?"

There was a note of irony in his voice. Everything he had just told me about the conspiracy – was I going to lay it out on the table among the bread and wine? Was he asking me to tell them about the agreement that Judas had made with Caiaphas? If the curtain were suddenly to be raised in this shadow theatre, wouldn't Peter and Iscariot come to blows? Wouldn't they rush and fetch their weapons from where they had left them by the door?

Was the celebration of the Kingdom going to end in a brawl?

53

Now there is nothing left to play for, I am sure I took the decision that had to be taken at that moment, and without delay. If I had exposed those who were behind the conspiracy, revealed everyone for what he really was, a sealed cauldron that was hovering at boiling point would have blown up in my face. The person in the most precarious position was Judas, who would find himself at the mercy of the activists whom he had betrayed. The most vital thing now was to protect him from their potentially violent reactions, especially Peter's. I had to tell him that I was aware of his plans, that he had my consent – but it had to be done in such a way that the others wouldn't realize; so they would think that I was telling him to go and buy what we needed for the festival, or to give something to the poor, as was the custom. He had to leave the room straight away.

I took a piece of bread and dipped it in the dish:

"It is the one to whom I give this piece of bread when I have dipped it in the dish."

Then I offered the piece of bread to Judas, who took it without a word. Looking him in the eye I whispered:

"Do quickly what you are going to do."

The others round the table were so astonished that when Judas got up and walked towards the door, his face expressionless, they didn't even react. As he went out he took his *sica* from the table and disappeared into the night.

When he had gone, I turned to Peter. In Galilee I had once accused him of being Satan; would those be the only words that would stay with him after tonight? No, he had to hear of hope and forgiveness, so he would know what God's loving kindness could be. So I spoke to him gently, using his pet name as his mother must have done when he was a child:

"Simon, Simon, listen! Satan has demanded to sift all of you like wheat! But I have prayed for you, Simon…"

Some of the disciples were defiant, perhaps they were finally beginning to understand. Was I going to be handed over? Well, they wouldn't let me be taken without a fight. They swung round and looked at the table by the door, where the two *sicas* could be seen among the coats.

"Rabbi, look, here are two swords!"

"It is enough," I replied. "My kingdom will not be won or held by force of arms, for all who take the sword will perish by the sword."

And I began to chant the Psalms of the *Hallel*, which brings the ritual to a close. Finally setting aside their differences, they joined in:

> The snares of death encompassed me,
> I suffered distress and anguish;
> O Lord, I pray, save my life!

When we left the house in the western part of the city, it was under cover of darkness and in sorrowful silence. The same as every night, we made our way to the Garden of Gethsemane to seek sanctuary; there were only eleven disciples now; the Judaean would meet us there later.

As we walked out of the room, I saw Peter pick up his *sica* and slip it under his coat.

54

I look up. The moon is now high in the sky; it must be the last watch before dawn. A blanket of silence seems to have descended on sleeping Jerusalem. Oh, those nights in Galilee when I would stand dreaming by the lake, watching the fishermen's lamps dance on the surface of the water! Leaning against an olive tree like I am tonight, I would sometimes stay till daybreak, waiting for them to come back so I could help unload the catch onto the shore. Often they would make a fire of thorn twigs and gently cook one or two fish in the embers, their delicate flesh flavoured by the sweet-smelling smoke.

How I wish I could relive those sensations, the smells, the brief conversations I had with passing strangers without giving it a second thought... During the last two years my every word has been scrutinized, evaluated, examined with the fine-tooth comb of ever-more merciless criticism, opposition and suspicion. In the coming light of dawn, why can't I simply wander back to my own home, open the door, ruffle the hair on my sleeping children's heads, smile at my wife as she lights the fire at the start of a new day? I feel such a need for tenderness, but all I can see is the granite wall of Jerusalem on which I am going to be broken.

Should I have ignored the call of the wilderness? I thought I had found a vocation, something that no ordinary Jew can turn his back on if he is to keep faith with his people. Where did it have its source, that commanding voice? In the madness that has been raging in Israel all these years, in my pride, or in God himself? And if it is God who is calling to me from within, then why choose me? *Why me?*

On the slope below the city wall, sharpened by hours of listening, my ears detect a new sound in the darkness: sandals crunching on the stony path, the tramp of marching feet, brief orders issued in a low voice. I leave the kindly embrace of the olive tree, while time flows by in the light of the stars. I lean forward and peer through the quivering foliage into the Kidron Valley, where now and then the light of torches can be seen flickering through the trees. They are heading this way, in single file.

The time has come.

I close my eyes. Suddenly I can barely breathe, the sound of my heartbeat is drumming inside my head. Let them come! *If I am only for myself, then who am I?* Once again, events are about to shape me into the man I am meant to be. A prophet doesn't live for *himself*, he lives for others; for his people. And, since my encounter with the Syrian woman and the centurion, for all the peoples.

But first there are my disciples to consider. If they are dragged from sleep by the sudden arrival of a squad of soldiers, how will they react? Will they run away, try to save themselves? Or will they put up a fight, will Peter draw his sword? And will he use it?

The torches are getting closer. Leaving the shelter of the tree, I walk slowly over to where they have made their camp. Once I have been handed over to Caiaphas, will he keep the oath he took? I don't believe that for a second. When I am at his mercy and he realizes that he can't convict me for blasphemy, he will use the first excuse he can think of to have me taken before Pilate.

And that means death.

After I am gone, will my Galileans finally become disciples? Or perhaps they will create an institution in my memory which will have nothing to do with what I was trying to be or to teach them, but which satisfies their desire for power?

When I get there they are already awake, standing in a huddle, peering anxiously into the valley. Little flock, how I have loved you despite everything... on the other side of the clearing, in the shadows beneath an olive tree I can make out the figure of the Judaean; so he is here too, as promised, loyal as ever. I know he will follow me to Caiaphas's palace – but after that there is nothing more he can do. My friend! He is the only one who simply tried to understand me, who asked nothing except to be allowed to hear the vast echo of my personal experience of God.

Everything has been fulfilled – or almost everything.

I am about to fight my last battle with Satan.

Have I managed to escape the Evil One's dance, am I finally free?

Once again I am alone in the presence of the Invisible, a naked prophet.

My God, my God, are you really going to forsake me?

Afterword

The fruit of thirty years of private research, these memoirs of an ordinary Jew also bear witness to a century of collective efforts with which I familiarized myself before even thinking of writing a word. The *quest for the historical Jesus*, which began in the nineteenth century, has worked its way through thousands of pages, as researchers advance from theories to provisional conclusions before coming to rest on a few established facts. We are no longer able to speak of Jesus, known as the Christ, in the way people spoke of him in the age of triumphant theology.

We now know a great deal more about the man himself than we did a century ago, thanks to the *demythologization* of the Gospels, which despite some excesses has enabled us to see the texts in a completely new light. Thanks, too, to archaeological work in the region, which provides Jewish life of the time with the essential third dimension that it has long been lacking. And last but not least, thanks to relentless study in many different fields: historiography, papyrology, linguistics, exegesis, sociology and comparative psychology have all helped explode the Christian myth. What was once unthinkable is now unavoidable – Jesus regarded as a historical figure and not a god.

The human substance of which dogma stripped him has now been restored.

Since Renan there have been countless versions of the "Life of Jesus", bogus autobiographies, novels ascribed to Pilate, Barabbas, Judas, Mary Magdalene and goodness knows who else... Not to mention the juicy and lucrative fantasies that claim to reveal his secret. Drowned in a sea of conflicting information and swollen by its tides, his corpse is now beyond recognition.

In 1995 I set out to write a study on his identity, with the help of those works that were then available in France.[1] Was he really God, as Christianity asserts?

This study gave rise to a thriller, which aimed to make some of the more recent discoveries available to a wider public.[2] In it I presented a mysterious thirteenth man, whose proximity to Jesus is no longer questioned. In order to complete my investigation into this unnamed Judaean, I attempted to unearth something that could be the echo of his eyewitness account, which has long lain buried in the text known as the Gospel According to John.[3]

This latest research eventually brought me to the foot of Everest – uncovering Jesus's own teaching from beneath the many words that have been put in his mouth.

Yet how was I to go about it? Should I add to the many thousands of pages already published by English, American, German, French and Jewish exegetical scholars? Plant another tree in an already dense forest?

---

1 This was published in 2001 as: *Dieu malgré lui, nouvelle enquête sur Jésus* (Robert Laffont).
2 First published in 2006 as *Le Secret du treizième apôtre* (Albin Michel), and since translated into eighteen languages. Published in English by Alma Books in 2007 as *The Thirteenth Apostle*.
3 This study is due to be published as *L'Évangile du treizième apôtre*.

Or instead, should I write another work of fiction on the life of Jesus, embellish it, use my imagination to fill the gaps in our knowledge?

While rereading Marguerite Yourcenar's *Memoirs of Hadrian*, I came across this comment: "One foot in scholarship, the other in that *magical empathy* which allows us to get inside another person's mind... And paint the portrait of a voice."

A woman from our own time shed her identity in order to think like a Roman emperor who died in the year 137. Rather than claiming to bring us the *sound of his voice*, she sketched out the *picture of a voice* that fell silent 1,800 years ago.

One foot in scholarship, the other in magical empathy... I had found the ice pick that would help me climb the slippery slope.

A portrait – but from which angle? Where should I set up my easel?

Some other words which Yourcenar attributes to Hadrian spring to mind: "I can just make out the figure of my approaching death." I had to find Jesus in the Garden of Gethsemane, during the night of utter solitude when he knows he is about to die and gives free rein to his memory.

He had to speak at the critical moment, the point when the pressure on him is at its greatest, when he realizes he is going to be put to death and yet is given a momentary reprieve – a device that enabled me to get round the insurmountable obstacle of chronology. It is a well-known fact that any biography of Jesus is doomed to failure, because each of the four Gospels, our best source of information, portrays events in its own particular way. Yet my research into John's Gospel led me to believe that in the most ancient section of the text, parts of the chronology were *reasonably* accurate, which allowed me to put some of the events that made up the Galilean's public life into a fairly reliable order.

Take the scandalous scene on the Temple esplanade, for example. Matthew, Mark and Luke site this at the end of their hero's career, viewing it as the spark that sets everything off. John, on the other hand, uses it as Jesus's first public act (the wedding at Cana being a family event). It poses no threat to his personal safety, which according to the Evangelist was only endangered after the healing of the man who was born blind and the raising of Lazarus – two incidents which take place quite close to each other in the original part of the Gospel.

So I put my trust in the rudimentary chronology of the Fourth Gospel. From the moment that Jesus leaves Judaea in order to put an end to the bickering between his disciples and those of John the Baptist, from the moment he starts travelling round Galilee and developing his own teaching, all chronology is lost. Only his visits to Jerusalem provide us with a few reliable landmarks.

Thus in the memory that I attribute to Jesus, events and conversations come back to him at random. As so often with our own past, he only remembers the most important things.

He was a man who experienced a process of inner gestation, only gradually becoming aware of himself and what he wanted to say. The Gospels bear witness to this in their accounts of his earliest discourses, which adhere closely to those of John the Baptist.

So when did he find himself? His teaching is presented to us as a whole, something that was formulated in his mind before he began his career as a preacher. Yet each of the four Evangelists arranges this material to suit his own ends. I have been inclined to follow Mark, who tends to be the least arbitrary in the way he distributes Jesus's discourses around the narrative.

To listen to a voice which can still be heard two thousand years later.

And Jesus's voice is unlike any other. Despite the centuries that separate us, despite the reworking carried out by the Gospel authors, there is a particular tone, a way of expressing himself that is common to all his parables and maxims. Research enables us to recreate this voice, or at least one that echoes the original as accurately as is possible.

As well as words there are also his acts. Considering the society in which he lived, his way of "moving" around the Jewish world strikes one as most original. It is evidence of an inner freedom that was very rare at the time.

The Gospels pay little attention to the emotions experienced by the main characters. In Jesus's case, there are a few surreptitious psychological clues – anger, disappointment, joy, sadness, tears... Yet we should beware of these peripheral touches, which don't reflect the Evangelists' usual mode of expression and certainly not their intentions. I only trust them when they are borne out by the context, the *Sitz im Leben*. Nonetheless, they offer little by way of indicators as to what someone at the centre of such tumultuous events must have really been feeling.

With regard to the conspiracy that led to Jesus's arrest and execution, my theory (with Peter as the main instigator and Judas shown to be innocent) is based on a careful reading of the New Testament. This goes against the official teaching. I will be glad to take criticism on this point, although on one condition: that all the sources are consulted, and none are passed over in silence.

What of the disciples?[4] We have only the slenderest of information on two of them – Peter, about whom all the witnesses lie

---

4 See my study of them, *Jésus et ses héritiers, mensonges et vérités* (Albin Michel, 2008).

by omission, and Judas, who is a victim of the most despicable vilification. If we compare the four Gospels, the Acts of the Apostles and Paul's Letters, we come to the conclusion that the Twelve never had the same aims as their rabbi (at least during his lifetime). Political designs, personal ambition, violence, treachery... the image of them that I hold up will only shock those who prefer, to the unsubtle light of the texts, a rosy myth which helps maintain their illusions.

That the disciples subsequently realized what they stood to gain from turning this man into a god is borne out by history itself. What is surprising is that the voice that has been so carefully muted by manufacturers of myths should have managed to reach us at all. If my attempt to paint his portrait succeeds, it is due to this voice's unparalleled robustness and originality.

It might surprise readers that I make no mention of the miracles involving the natural world which are ascribed to Jesus[5] – but exegetical scholars have serious reservations as to their historical accuracy. His powers of healing, however, are confirmed by sound factual evidence. My interpretation of this – the confluence of a strong desire to heal with the qualities of a thaumaturge – rules out the possibility of magic while still not offering a satisfactory answer to rationalists. This is because they tend to overlook something that medicine is only now beginning to rediscover: that every illness is essentially an affliction of the soul, or (to use the correct terminology) a psychosomatic disorder. If called upon to do so, our mental powers are able to repair, either wholly or in part, any defects in our body. For those trapped inside a mechanistic view of the human condition, the power of healing displayed by a shaman or a Jesus figure can only be explained as a miracle or a hoax.

---

5 Walking on water, miraculous catches of fish, stilling the storm, the withered fig tree.

"We civilizations have come to realize that we are mortal." After an extraordinarily long life, Christianity is experiencing a dramatic decline. The great mother tree is only held up by its bark, its leaves drift down onto a soil that is now indifferent to them. Robbed of its age-old roots, the West (which was once Christian) is also suffering from an identity crisis the like of which it has never known before.

Is it possible to give him back his vital force, which was lost at the same moment that Christianity itself collapsed? The various Churches have proved themselves incapable of this task. They have silenced prophets and theologians alike, leaving only a race of preceptors.

At the beginning of the first century AD, established Judaism was also spent, divided, unable to adapt, using up what remained of its strength in order to survive in a hostile or indifferent world. The Nazarene, however, was guided by a fundamental intuition: to return to the *original source*, to leave the Moses of Sinai and the Law behind and rediscover the Moses of the Burning Bush.

To go beyond the Law without disregarding it.

Witnesses as we are to the inexorable decline of a Catholic Church that is fossilized in its past, paralysed by dogma and with nothing to say to a world in the grip of a spiritual drought, are we able to follow his example? To go back to the *original source* of the vast Christian edifice and hear the voice of the Prophet of Galilee as if for the first time, aware that he was betrayed from the start by the very individuals who handed down his memory to us after hiding it beneath a heavy mask?[6]

Are we able to unmask Christ? The *quest for the historical Jesus* now provides us with the means of doing so.

---

6 For the question of origins, see *Jésus et ses héritiers* (Albin Michel, 2008).

It offers perspectives that strike a chord with our own age.

Optimism. Jesus never attempted to change the world, he proclaimed its end. He is the very first member of the alter-globalization movement, sketching out the beginnings of a new world in which happiness is a basic human right.

Suffering. He rejects the belief that it is inevitable. Whenever he encounters it, he never reacts with indifference. For him, no hopeless situation is permanent, not illness, not death (which is just an outward appearance), not sin – which during his lifetime was the main reason for social exclusion.

Compassion. He is steeped in it, unceasingly and to his very depths. It removes all barriers erected by tradition, laws, social customs and personal interests. Completely open to his neighbours, he allows himself to be permeated by them. In this way a new social order is created, whose principal concern is that everyone should be able to fulfil their own individual calling.

Women. If they are equal to men, this is not as a result of pitying them, but rather an acknowledgement of the first act of creation, which cannot continue to be disregarded. Created to be man's partner, woman joins with him in seeking the harmony of the first man and woman in a shared pleasure that offers a foretaste of the Kingdom.

Sexuality. Unlike the members of its elite, traditional ancient society displayed a severe moral attitude. On meeting a prostitute or a woman who has committed adultery, Jesus sees only a human being on the road to love, which is one stage in the journey of complete self-fulfilment.

Active non-violence. More than any other prophet (and long before Gandhi), he was the first to suggest this as the answer to both individual and collective disputes.

He was also the first to introduce the idea of a *secular society.* Since God is in heaven, he cannot be called upon to justify laws and customs that are in conflict with the law of the heart.

And the first to establish an *ethics of intent*, by rejecting the suggestion, when faced with the man who was born blind, that a curse or *original sin* hangs over all of us from the moment of our birth. We alone are responsible for our actions, as well as the consequences that may arise from them.

Meditation. I can think of no other word to describe his way of praying, which was unheard of in Judaism, and was met with surprise and a total lack of understanding by those closest to him. He never shared the secret of this private, inner world, although from what we are able to tell it was not dissimilar to the practice used in Hindu-Buddhism.

In all of the above, Jesus appears to be surprisingly close to Siddhārtha Gautama, the Buddha.[7] The world's truly Awakened Ones all share the same experience, and in its essence their teaching is virtually identical.

To attempt to summarize his teaching in a few words would be to betray him a second time. During the period he spent in the wilderness, this man had a direct experience of God's presence that was so insistent that he was only able to convey it by means of a series of blinding intuitions (hence the seeming lack of order in the Gospels). Like all human beings, he is ultimately beyond analysis. It is left to the reader to look beyond the words and try to gain an insight into their own heart, which is the only thing that enables human beings to understand each other.

In our efforts to find him we run up against one major obstacle: he created no organization that would continue with his work. Like the prophets who came before him, he understood the limitations

---

7 On this subject see Part 2 of *Dieu malgré lui* (Robert Laffont, 2001), 'Un Bouddha juif' ('A Jewish Buddha').

of religious institutions and roundly condemned them. Truly *anti-clerical*, he was happy simply to sow the seeds.

Which is why a church of any kind can only betray him.

So what does the future hold for his personal teaching? Are those over whom he still exercises a fascination destined to remain a small group of nameless individuals lost among the vast majority who cannot manage without myths or dogma? Is this not what he was trying to say in his first parable, when he pointed out that very few seeds take root and grow, and then almost by chance?

Can we ever catch hold of these seeds, which blow on the wind in a world buffeted by storms?

Main Gospel References

The following abbreviations are used for the books of the Old and New Testaments:

Mk: Mark. Mt: Matthew. Lk: Luke. Jn: John. Acts: Acts of the Apostles. Ps: Psalms (Hebrew numbering). Lev: Leviticus.

The sign // refers to parallels between the synoptic Gospels – Matthew, Mark and Luke.

For the English translation, the biblical quotations are based on the New Revised Standard Edition of the Bible (Anglicized text), 2003, translated from the Hebrew, Aramaic and Greek.

*

Ch 1:	Mk 14:32 & //. Jn 11:57. Mt 26:40 & //. Mk 8:28 & //; 8:31; 9:31; 10:33 & //. Jn 11:8; 12:4; 13:26
Ch 2:	Mk 14:70. Lk 13:32. Mk 6:3. Lk 4:22 & Jn 1:45; 6:42. Acts 1:14
Ch 3:	Jn 21:3. Mt 2:13–15
Ch 4:	Lk 16:17 & //. Mt 5:19; 22:36 & //
Ch 5:	Mk 7:3–4
Ch 6:	Lk 7:34
Ch 7:	Mk 1:4 & //; 6:18 & //. Mt 3:7–10. Lk 3:10–14; 3:5; 3:4. Lk 4:16 & //
Ch 8:	Mk 1:4–6 & //

Ch 9:   Mk 1:12–13 & //
Ch 10:   Mt 3:14. Jn 1:26 & //. Jn 1:37–39; 19:23; 1:42–50; 3:29
Ch 11:   Jn 4:21; 2:1–10
Ch 12:   Mk 1:21–26 & //. Lk 4:18; 4:21–22
Ch 13:   Jn 1:44. Mk 1:29. Mt 4:21–22. Mk 3:17. Acts 4:13. Mk 1:29–31 & //; 1:32–37 & //
Ch 14:   Mt 4:17 & //. Mk 1:40–45 & //
Ch 15:   Mk 2:1–12 & //. Jn 2:13–15. See Acts 21:27–32
Ch 16:   Jn 2:23; 3:1–4; 3:22–26; 3:30; 4:1–3; 4:4–40. Mt 23:4
Ch 17:   Mk 5:30. Lk 7:11–15. Mt 9:16
Ch 18:   Mk 3:13–14; 2:35–37; 6:31 & //; 2:13–17 & //
Ch 19:   Mk 2:23–27; 3:1–6
Ch 20:   Mk 3:20; 3:31–35; 3:21; 3:22–26 & //; 6:4; 17
Ch 21:   Jn 11:18. Lk 10:38–40. Jn 5:2–15
Ch 22:   Lk 7:18–22 & //. Mt 14:1–11 & //. Mt 9:17
Ch 23:   Mt 5:13–16. Mk 4:2–9 & //; 4:14–20 & //; 4:13
Ch 24:   Jn 13:29
Ch 25:   Mt 5:3–10 & //; 5:21–22 & //
Ch 26:   Mk 5:1–17 & //; 5:21–43 & //
Ch 27:   Mt 5:38–45; 5:33–35. Lk 7:36–50 & //
Ch 28:   Mk 6:7–12 & //. Lk 10:18. Mk 6:30–43 & //; 6:45
Ch 29:   Lk 6:12. Ps 139:4. Ps 131:2. Mk 9:2–4 & //; 9:14–29 & //. Mk 8:17
Ch 30:   Mk 7:1–23 & //
Ch 31:   Mk 7:24–30 & //. Mk 8:27–33 & //; 10:32 & //
Ch 32:   Lk 8:2–3; 10:38–42. Mk 15:43 & //. Lk 22:39. Mk 10:13–15 & //. Jn 7:1
Ch 33:   Mk 3:9. Mt 22:1–10 & //; 25:1–10; 13:44; 13:24–30. Mk 9:1. Mt 13:33; 31–32. Mk 9:33–36 & //
Ch 34:   Mt 8:5–13 & //. Lk 7:1–10
Ch 35:   Mk 8:11–13 & //. Lk 11:20 & //. Mt 13:16–17 & //. Lk 11:1–4 & //. Mt 6:5–8

Ch 36: Jn 7:2; 7:3–4; 7:9–10; 8:1; 8:2–11; 8:59

Ch 37: Jn 9:1–34. Mt 21:17. Jn 10:40

Ch 38: Mk 10:1–12 & //

Ch 39: Mk 12:28–34 & //. Lk 10:29–37. Mk 10:13–16 & //. Lk 13:31

Ch 40: Lk 15:11–24. Mk 10:33–34 & //; 10:35–43 & //. Mt 20:20

Ch 41: Mt 8:19–20. Mk 10:17–27 & //. Mt 19:24–26

Ch 42: Ps 19:2. Jn 11:3; 11:6; 11:7–8. Mt 23:37 & //. Lk 9:51

Ch 43: Mk 10:32. Lk 19:1–8. Mk 10:46–52. Mk 11:1–10 & //

Ch 44: Jn 11:17; 11:19–23; 11:31–39; 11:41; 11:43–44. Acts 4:2. Jn 18:15

Ch 45: Jn 12:2–3; 12:7; 12:4–5; 12:8; 12:9; 11:46–53; 7:50–52; 11:57; 12:10–11; 7:49; 11:54

Ch 46: Lk 23:46. Jn 11:55–56. Lk 22:39; 22:10 & //

Ch 47: Jn 19:23. Mk 12:18–27 & //. Mk 13:1–4

Ch 48: Mk 12:13–17 & //; 12:35–37 & //

Ch 49: Lk 22:38 & Jn 18:10. Mk 12:41–44

Ch 50: Mk 14:13 & //; 14:15 & //. Acts 5:28; 5:40. Mt 26:15 & //. Lev 27:2–8. Jn 18:15–16

Ch 51: Mk 1:29; 5:37; 9:2 & //; 10:35. Acts 1:18. Lk 9:54. Jn 13:4–15

Ch 52: Mk 14:22–25 & //. Lk 22:24. Jn 13:21–25

Ch 53: Jn 13:26–30. Lk 22:31–32; 22:38. Mt 26:52. Ps 116a:3–4

Ch 54: Jn 21:9. Mk 14:50. Jn 18:10; 19:30. Mt 27:46 & //

BY THE SAME AUTHOR:

THE THIRTEENTH APOSTLE
75,000 COPIES SOLD IN UK

TRANSLATED BY ANDREW BROWN

When his friend, Father Andrei, is mysteriously killed on a train on his way back from Rome, Father Nil decides to conduct his own investigation. The dead priest possessed proof of the existence of a thirteenth apostle and an epistle stating that Jesus was nothing more than an inspired prophet, not the Son of God – two things that would spell great danger for the Church.

While he pushes ahead with his investigation, the Pope's advisors, rival factions and secret societies are trying, by any means, to lay their hands on the priest's findings. From the Mossad to Fatah, everyone seems to have a very good reason to keep the thirteenth apostle a secret...

384 pp • £7.99 • 9781846881534
eBook • £7.99 • 9781846881206

PRISONER OF GOD
THE INTERNATIONAL BESTSELLER

TRANSLATED BY ROGER CLARKE

A brilliant student with a promising career ahead of him as a biologist, Michel Benoît decided at the age of twenty-two to follow the path of God and take on monastic orders as Brother Irénée. But after more than twenty years of self-sacrifice and a fraught quest for God, Michel was "discharged" by the Church. What happened? What led to the Catholic hierarchy rejecting one of its own?

Prisoner of God is a compelling examination of sectarianism and the methods used by organizations to stifle freedom of expression and crush the individual. It is also an account of the mysterious world of the abbeys: the monks' everyday life and the way they deal with solitude, silence and sexuality.

288 pp. • £8.99 • 9781846880520